METROPOLITAN PLACES

METROPOLI

VIKING
STUDIO
BOOKS

TAN PLACES

TEXT AND PHOTOGRAPHS BY

ELIZABETH HEYERT

DESIGN BY LOUISE FILI · STYLING BY CARLA CAPALBO

VIKING STUDIO BOOKS

Published by the Penguin Group
Viking Penguin, a division of Penguin Books USA Inc.,
40 West 23rd Street, New York, N.Y. 10010, USA

Penguin Books Ltd, 27 Wrights Lane,
London W8 5TZ, England

Penguin Books Australia Ltd, Ringwood,
Victoria, Australia

Penguin Books Canada Ltd, 2801 John Street,
Markham, Ontario, Canada L3R 1B4

Penguin Books (N.Z.) Ltd, 182-190 Wairau Road,
Auckland 10, New Zealand

Penguin Books Ltd, Registered Offices:
Harmondsworth, Middlesex, England

First published in 1989 by Viking Penguin,
a division of Penguin Books USA Inc.
Published simultaneously in Canada

10   9   8   7   6   5   4   3   2   1

LIBRARY OF CONGRESS CATALOGING IN PUBLICATION DATA
Heyert, Elizabeth.
    Metropolitan places / Elizabeth Heyert.
        p.   cm.
    ISBN 0-670-81743-0 :
    1. Interior decoration—History—20th
century.   2. Interior architecture.
3. Apartments.   I. Title.
NK1980.H49   1989
728′.314′0904—dc20   88-40632

Printed in Japan
Set in Perpetua

F O R   D O U G

C O N T E N T S

A C K N O W L E D G M E N T S

Much of the credit for this book must go to my wonderful crew, a group of women whose creativity, enthusiasm, skill, and style made this project the extraordinary experience it was. My gratitude to Carla Capalbo, stylist, translator, and dear friend, is immeasurable—for her exquisite attention to detail and elegant sense of restraint, her seemingly limitless energy for even the most thankless tasks that somehow made all the difference to a photograph, for her ability to conduct the most obscure conversations in flawless French, and for her unswerving belief in the book and in me. Her generosity with her time and her talent made it possible for me to do what often seemed, and without her might have been, impossible. Many, many thanks to Caterina Borelli, my Italian and Spanish translator who became a friend somewhere between Milan and Barcelona, for her skillful interpretation of difficult questions, her whirlwind energy, remarkable efficiency, humor, and spirit, and for her special sensitivity to the content and quality of the design in each city. As for Monica Buck, my photo assistant, who hauled equipment from city to city and continent to continent, kept track of three hundred rolls of film at once, soothed irate customs officials in Berlin in perfect German and in Mexico in perfect Spanish, and never once lost her temper or her concentration, my special thanks—how would I have done it without you? The talent of these three women, all artists in their own right, penetrates every page of this book.

To my agent, Lucy Kroll, heartfelt thanks for having confidence in me and my work from the very first day, and for sharing with me her vision of the roads I might travel with my photography and my writing. Also, many thanks to Barbara Hogenson, whose unswerving interest and commitment to my book were there from the start of the project, and who made every step easier because of her scrupulous and thoughtful participation. My thanks to the team at Viking Studio Books, especially Michael Fragnito—for his constant belief in this book and for the support that made the project possible—and my editor, Barbara Williams, whose meticulous attention to my manuscript as well as her commitment to the integrity of the project added immeasurably to its quality. My thanks also to Louise Fili for her sensitive design and her understanding of the pictures and of the places, and especially for so generously allowing me to participate in the delicate design process.

For their advice and valuable participation I would like to thank Jed Johnson, Nancy Kintisch, Laurie Parks, Christopher Hodsill, Lili Verame, Gae Aulenti, Michele Curel, Professor Juan Bassegoda Nonell, Odile Fillon, Eva Jiricna, Anna Castelli, Douce Francois, Aldo Cibic, Adrian Ward-Jackson, Steven Earle,

Anne Lamouche, Gilly Newbury, Matthew Rice, Henrietta Green, Julyan Wickham, Sandra Lousada, Luli Shoei, Kendell Lutkins, Fred Hughes, Nanette Boralevi, Carla Stellweg, Shelia Klein, Quim Larrea, Nuna Smith, Maria Pena, Elena Bellini, Gary Ebbins, Albert Hadley, Helen Wright, John Taras, Isabelle Lousada, Anthony Brown, Lady Sainsbury, Nancy Norman Lassalle, Penny Maguire, Dulio Gregorini, Santiago Miranda, Perry King, Anna Castelli, Vico Magistretti, Barbara Radice, Salome, Juli Capella, Xavier Carulla, Bartomeu Cruells, Joan Boivin, and all the architects, designers, and owners of homes in each city who generously allowed us into their apartments, houses, palazzos, lofts, and studios.

Special thanks to my friends and family, whose involvement with this book and support during my struggles to complete it were invaluable to me. My wonderful friend and colleague Richard Horn, who shared my fascination with city rooms long before this project was committed to paper, died in the spring of 1989, six months before his thirty-fifth birthday. His unique perceptions about the subtle machinations of design communities around the world had always been a revelation to me, but I am especially grateful for the companionship, unswerving enthusiasm, and the sympathetic (often acerbically funny) words of advice and encouragement that he provided in abundance all through the writing of this book, in spite of his long illness. Much of what I know about design I learned from Richard. My warm thanks to Rob Reiner, whose reassurance was endless and essential, who managed the nearly impossible task of getting me to laugh when the pressure was on, and who made me believe that maybe I would, in spite of myself, finish the book. Many thanks to Mette Albers, who acted as translator and guide in Berlin, and who, with her husband, Michael, led me to the heart of that remarkable city and helped me to understand it. Also, my gratitude to Sir Anthony and Lady Lousada for their invaluable assistance with the difficult process of location scouting in both Europe and America, which enabled me to expand the project into worlds that otherwise would have been closed to me, and for their generosity in providing friendship, advice, and a cozy refuge in London. Thanks to my dear London friends Milena and David Bentheim for the abundant amounts of tea and sympathy they offered after a hard day's shoot. And my deepest thanks to my father, who taught me how to use a camera and how to write an essay.

Finally, to my husband, Doug, who lived with the project day and night for two years, listened to every version of every one of my essays, and whose challenging and perceptive suggestions often made a great, great difference, I lovingly dedicate this book.

I N T R O D U C T I O N

Metropolitan Places is about my travels to eight cities to see how people who have the luxury of choice design their homes. Unlike most people who live in cities, the people whose homes appear in this book have not had their living circumstances thrust upon them. They live in apartments or lofts or studios or palazzos or town houses or even in converted factories in preference to country cottages or houses in the suburbs. However, this is not a book solely about the way the very rich or the very famous live, even though many of the people whose homes appear here are rich and, in some cases, famous. While some of these interiors have never been seen before by the public, others are better known and more celebrated than their owners. What the homes in the book have in common, besides their city location, is that each one expresses a completely original vision. Each of these interiors is like no other in the world.

This book took approximately two years to complete. Almost one-third of that time was devoted to selecting the cities and homes. Initially, I planned to photograph interiors in a wide variety of cities, especially in the United States. I assumed that, like the extraordinary homes I knew in New York, Paris, and London, great interiors could also be found—flavored with some interesting regional variations—in most major American cities. To my surprise, I found that in many cities it was difficult to find any home, except perhaps for an isolated example bearing little relation to the design climate of the city, that did not resemble countless others. In the end I let the quality of design that naturally emerged from each city determine my choice. I did extensive research; read back issues of various design magazines to get an idea of the best and, more often, the very worst residential interior design; and saw many more locations than I would eventually photograph. Any home that looked as if a decorator had predetermined a style and then applied it to a place without regard for the location, architecture, or personality of the owner was immediately eliminated. On the other hand, I sought out interiors by certain great decorators, like Geoffrey Bennison and Renzo Mongiardino, both so widely imitated that I wanted to document original examples of their work. The same is true for the great architects whose work is included in this book—Luis Barragán, Frank Lloyd Wright, Antonio Gaudí. Whether or not an interior had been published before was not a concern. My criteria for selection were originality and timelessness.

Of course, some of my reasons for selecting one city over another were subjective. New York, London, Paris, and Los Angeles were obvious choices. Instead of Rome, I chose Milan—because of its unique status as a city whose leading industry is design. I decided to see how four masters—a pioneer

furniture designer, a celebrated fashion designer, and two important designers whose interiors are from the opposite ends of the design spectrum—created homes for themselves. I chose Barcelona rather than Madrid because it best represents the "new Spain" emerging creatively after forty years of fascism, and also because of its continuing tradition of artistic innovation as best exemplified in the extraordinary buildings of the Catalan visionary architect Antonio Gaudí. Mexico City, not usually on the short list of world design centers, was chosen for a different reason—because the great Luis Barragán created many of his masterworks there, and the best of the city and of Mexican culture seemed to me to be embodied in his architecture. My great regret is not having had the time or resources to include Tokyo, which has emerged in the last few years as a major center for important design.

To say that each city included here has its own design character would be making too broad a generalization. I am reluctant to attribute a "city style" to a specific location, especially because each of the interiors represented here is so distinctively the result of an individual's personal sensibility. However, I was fascinated to discover that sometimes politics and the intellectual climate of a particular city could influence design decisions. For example, try to imagine the interior of the White House in Washington, D.C., or of 10 Downing Street in London being renovated by avant-garde designers the next time a conservative administration is replaced by liberals. Yet, in Paris, that was basically President Mitterrand's intention when he commissioned Philippe Starck and other young French designers to transform the ornate rooms installed in the Elysée Palace by Georges Pompidou into a radical modern environment. In West Berlin, the circumstances of that city's existence—surrounded by the East, isolated from the West, and confronted with the ever-present threat of nuclear destruction—are reflected in much of its art and certainly in its interior design. On the first day of my location scout there, I asked through my translator if the owner of the house we were visiting could suggest another place for me to see. "Oh yes," he said. "You must see the home of my friend. It is extremely brutal. Quite violent." It took me a few moments to realize that in West Berlin design circles this was the highest recommendation.

I never forced a theme out of any city, and tried to avoid imposing my own editorial slant. In fact, the design told its own story. In London, in all but one of the homes I photographed, the design is a variation on the theme of English ornamentation, from the traditional nineteenth-century opulence of the Goldsmith and Nevill interiors to the decorative symbolism of Jencks and the abstract expressionism of

Pirroni. The other, John Pawson's interior, reflects a trend toward the extreme opposite, and is a good example of the spare architecture being created by a new generation of London architects in reaction to the English decorative tradition. In Barcelona, traditional values coexist with radical ideas in almost every aspect of daily life, so it is not surprising to find a delicate balance between the old and the new Spain reflected in interior design. In Los Angeles, the irreverence for tradition combined with a willingness to experiment that is characteristic of the best aspects of that city can be seen in the design of the three houses included here. My greatest challenge was selecting homes in New York, where I live and work, and where the smorgasbord of interior design is abundant and overwhelming. It is a city where there is often a sense that who you are can be, and in fact must be, created—by the style you adopt, and by whom and what you surround yourself with. When Andy Warhol chose to live with nineteenth- and twentieth-century antiques in a town house on the Upper East Side of Manhattan, he was making a statement about his success and his status as much as selecting a decor or a neighborhood. Dan Friedman goes so far as to refer to the walls of his apartment as a "diary"—of his ever-changing moods and emotions as much as of his evolving design sensibility. You might say that his apartment is an advertisement for himself and his work, a grand-scale illustration of the way he would like to be perceived. The New York homes included here are, in many respects, the "stage dressing" their owners show to the world.

Photography for this project began in London and Paris, where we shot all twelve interiors in a whirlwind three weeks, and ended, eight months later, in Mexico City. We spent a lot of time on airplanes and not very much time in our hotel rooms. We ate hasty lunches surrounded by the chic fashion crowd in Milan and late-night dinners in cramped student cafés in Barcelona. We traveled with ten cases of cameras and lighting equipment in addition to our own luggage. Much of what we experienced during that time does not appear in the photographs but has left a lasting impression—seeing the view of the Seine through the tall windows of Rudolf Nureyev's apartment, the momentary silence among us at the first sight of the strong yellow light that flooded the entrance of Luis Barragán's final interior, the shock of turning a corner in West Berlin and seeing the Wall. Sometimes, while exposing film or while waiting for the light, we would debate back and forth about what city and what interior we would most like to live in. Our ideas changed from city to city and from room to room. Even now, looking back after some months have passed, it is a difficult choice to make.

N E W   Y O R K

G I L L E T T E

"The world can be hard on you," says Rick Gillette, a well-known makeup artist who lives in a loft high above the twisting maze of New York's financial district. "In New York, especially this part of New York," he says, gesturing toward the skyscraper view outside his penthouse windows, "I am surrounded by harshness. Up here I can shelter myself in an aura of peace, even if it is a bit unreal." For eight years Gillette had lived in a dramatic, much-publicized Deco-style apartment on Park Avenue. "That was part of a childhood fantasy for me," he says. "You know the song 'Let's Go Slumming on Park Avenue'? I always knew I would move." The Wall Street area fascinated Gillette because of the intense activity surrounding the financial world, so far removed from the fashion scene he is a part of. He also liked the idea of living so close to the water. "Down here," Gillette says, "you realize that you are living on an island."

Several years ago he answered a newspaper ad that promised "a cabin in the sky." The advertised space was a long, narrow hall with twelve offices running down the length of a building, and a network of exposed water pipes lining the ceiling. To Gillette, who immediately envisioned the space with the walls torn down and the offices removed, the architecture was reminiscent of "a Gothic church—except for the pipes—with a main altar and four chapels." Gillette, who has always been drawn to Gothic architecture, and at one time considered buying a church, began an ambitious program of renovation to transform the offices, along the lines of his own vision, with the help of the California architect Frank Israel. Gillette wanted to create small areas within larger ones, similar to the small chapels within large Gothic cathedrals. "Then," says Gillette, "I saw a book about Luis Barragán. I decided to have a Barragán-style village within a Gothic structure."

Originally, Gillette used colors in the loft often associated with Barragán, such as vibrant terra cotta on a wall that he has since painted over in a more somber forest green. As the project developed, Gillette became more interested in interpreting, rather than mimicking, Barragán's ideas in ways that would relate to his own. Water, an essential element in every Barragán space, was important to Gillette also. "I remembered seeing photographs in *Life* magazine of Venice after it had been flooded. I wanted my place to look as if it were sitting in water." The concrete floors were painted iridescent blue "to look like water over dirt." A fountain, with a trough in the Barragán style, surrounded by a Gothic-style vaulted ceiling and a stained-glass window, pours water into a bath pool, which to Gillette is the source that "begins the flood for the entire house." He has carried out this fantasy to such an extent that the pool is designed to overflow into a carefully concealed gutter at its base, which catches excess water before it can actually do damage.

Gillette's home is his passion. He devotes much of his spare time to making what appears to an outside observer to be infinitesimal changes to an already exceptional space. Most likely Gillette left his Park Avenue apartment, with its muraled walls and Cubist painted doorways, because it was finally perfect— nothing more could be done to improve it. Now Gillette is in the process of acquiring American mission furniture for his loft and constructing another "chapel." When that is done, and the project is finally finished, chances are he'll look for another home.

Right: Gillette's idea for the seating area was to use "furniture as pieces of art." The early mission chair in the foreground is English, from the end of the nineteenth century, with modern upholstery. The couches are covered with African cloths made in the Ivory Coast from hand-woven cotton and painted with mud dye. The lamp is American mission style.

Left: The niche, one of a pair located in the hall, was designed to resemble a confessional. From the hall, one can see into the court-yard and beyond to a fire-place surrounded by a seating area.

Right: The influence of Luis Barragán can most clearly be seen in the plain stair without a rail, similar to the stair in Barragán's own Mexico City home. The structure behind the stair, which is at the center of the loft, is described by Gillette as "a building within a building, with a courtyard in front of it." To the right of the stair is a sliding gate that separates the courtyard from the hall. The stair leads to a small room intended as a study but currently used as a storage area.

Far right: The idea for a bathing pool filled by water cascading from a trough was inspired by the pools of Luis Barragán, and designed to simulate the feeling of showering outside. This pool is actually a Jacuzzi. A conventional shower is located in a niche in the left wall adjacent to the pool. The pipes were a part of the original architecture that has been allowed to remain. The angel sculpture is a nineteenth-century garden statue.

R O T H S C H I L D

"The apartment that started it all" is the way one decorator reacted to the mention of the New York apartment of Baron Guy de Rothschild and his wife, Marie-Hélène. By "it all" he meant the famous Rothschild look, *le style Rothschild,* a term that in current decorating circles needs no further explanation. It is a style of decorating that found favor in New York in the money- and status-conscious 1980s. Decorators new to the scene have grown famous by imitating it. For Marie-Hélène Rothschild, the design and decoration of the apartment, which she describes as "comfortable and cozy," a place where she likes to go "after shopping or some other engagement," were merely extended from the European homes she has established elsewhere.

There are endless stories about the homes of the Rothschilds, which is not surprising given that the wealth and power of the family span almost two centuries. One story has it that after Mayer Rothschild built Mentmore, an enormous late-nineteenth-century English country house with turrets and towers and other architectural extravagances, his brother James immediately contacted his own architect. "Build another Mentmore, only twice the size," he is supposed to have said, with the result that the château in Ferrières, outside Paris, was created. Many of the pieces in the Rothschilds' New York apartment came from the château at Ferrières, since, says Marie-Hélène, she enjoys having her possessions around her wherever she goes. After looking at dozens of apartments, Marie-Hélène thought this one, with its twenty-foot ceiling in the living room, was atypical of New York and had a European feel. She went to work with the famous English decorator Geoffrey Bennison, to create an atmosphere closely approaching the traditional European style she is comfortable with. Apparently, the apartment was a complete surprise to her husband, who expected a modern, sleek New York environment, but Marie-Hélène's preference is "not to stay within the style of a city." The Baron, she says, was responsible for the decoration of the house in Morocco.

Bennison worked intensely on the apartment for eight months. He imported his own group of artisans from Europe—upholsterers, painters, stencilers, joiners, and carpenters—his well-known "family," who worked on all his elaborate projects, including the London home he decorated for Isabel Goldsmith. The walls were painted faux bois, then stenciled to look like marquetry, in a pattern inspired by Hever Castle, in England, which had belonged, at one time, to the Astors. Bennison made countless trips to Ferrières with Marie-Hélène, applying his remarkable "eye" to a century's accumulation of art and antiques, and picking and choosing with great care. "Geoffrey was very imaginative and talented," says Marie-Hélène, whose Paris home was decorated by Bennison's rival and peer Renzo Mongiardino. "His use of color and fabric was extraordinary. But his great gift was playing things down. I loved that about him." The result was a gorgeous blend of furniture upholstered with lush, old tapestries collected by Bennison over a thirty-year period, cozy ottomans covered with Bennison's prized nineteenth-century Ziegler carpets, old lace, William Morris curtains, priceless antiques from Ferrières, and nineteenth-century Indian crewelwork, all mixed together with the insouciance for which Bennison is justly renowned. A designer who worked with Bennison before he died explained the Rothschild apartment this way: "One feels relaxed and cozy there, and it all seems familiar, welcoming, and accessible. It never feels like a museum. Geoffrey rises to the grandeur and style of the architecture, and the quality of the antiques and objects, but with all that he made it livable." For Marie-Hélène, the apartment is a haven, "a contrast to the harsh environment of New York." For Bennison's imitators, his gift for understatement in the face of great wealth is a natural talent which eludes all but the most astute.

Left: The walls of the living room were painted faux bois and then stenciled to look like inlaid wood. The fabric on the upper walls is Tulip Border, a Bennison design that was specially colored for this apartment. The sofas are nineteenth-century, from the Rothschild château at Ferrières. The cushions are covered in nineteenth-century needlework collected by Bennison. The red chair is a mock-Victorian design by Bennison covered in antique material found at Ferrières. On the fireplace mantel and over the door to the library are seventeenth-century Urbino apothecary jars from Ferrières. The floor rug and the upholstery on the center ottoman are nineteenth-century Ziegler carpets. The painting on the left is a portrait of Baron Alphonse de Rothschild, the grandfather of the current owner, painted by Aimé Morot. The chandelier is seventeenth-century Dutch. The eighteenth-century Roman Empire colored marble busts are two of a set of four from the Great Hall at Ferrières. The seventeenth-century Dutch ebony mirror, which appeared large when purchased, was dwarfed by the huge scale of the room. Bennison had the mirror enlarged, a difficult technical feat.

Above: The rare French clock was made by Boulle of tortoise shell and gold. The table is covered by a Ziegler carpet. All the ceramics on the table are German. The lace curtains are from the collection at Ferrières. The draperies are made from pieces of William Morris tapestry and Bennison fabric designed to match, a technique Bennison often used to increase the volume of the scarce William Morris material. Bennison used the same technique in the London apartment created for Isabelle Goldsmith.

*Left: The gilt bed is Second
Empire, in the Rococo
style. The linen fabric on
the walls is a Bennison design called Brown Roses.
The eighteenth-century
chair on the left is covered
with antique tapestry from
Ferrières. The table is a
late-eighteenth-century
worktable from England.
The small sofa along the
far wall was upholstered by
Bennison with strips of velvet alternating with pieces
of nineteenth-century needlepoint. The rug is nine-
teenth-century.*

Right: The walls of the dining room are covered with pieces of nineteenth-century Indian crewelwork from Bennison's private collection, as is the table-cloth. The tiger is nineteenth-century English needlework. The candle-sticks are eighteenth-century French. The green enamel and gilt bronze rotary clock, entitled The Three Graces, is Louis XVI with movement by Lepante. At its top is a cupid with an arrow that points to the numerals.

Left: Around the fireplace in the library are eighteenth-century Delft tiles, similar to the tiles later used in the Goldsmith apartment. Above it is an ebony and mahogany mirror. To the left is a painting attributed to Boucher. The two nineteenth-century armchairs are from Ferrières. The writing table is late-eighteenth-century English. The book table in the foreground is nineteenth-century. The needlepoint chair is a Bennison design. The carpet is Ziegler.

M A L L E T

"Memories floating out of the wall plane" is the way Alison Sky of the architecture firm SITE describes her conception for Laurie Mallet's nineteenth-century house in the heart of Greenwich Village. Mallet, the president of the WilliWear clothing company, lives on a winding tree-lined street reminiscent of her native Paris. Mallet, who previously lived in a loft, wanted a home where she could coexist comfortably with her two children and a nanny and still have room to express her own sensibilities, which lean toward the arts and the avant-garde. The house she found had been untouched by the previous owners for twenty-five years. She showed the place to several of the architects at SITE, who immediately responded to the charming character of the street and the elegant proportions of the house as well as to the aura of history and the echoes of previous inhabitants that seemed to resonate from its walls. In spite of the dark, tiny rooms and the fact that the house, according to Sky, "had nothing unique about detailing, and no precious materials had been used," Sky and her associates were determined to preserve a relationship with the past, the "historical layering" that remained in the feel of the place, if not in the structure itself.

From the early days of the project, the pasts of the house and of the new owner would guide almost every creative decision. "We were determined," says Sky, "not to make the house into something it was never intended to be." Although the house had to be gutted before renovation could begin, the architects saved as many pieces of the original architecture as they could and preserved them as part of their unique design program. An original door frame stands alone, without walls, in the living room, a solitary reminder that at one time that space was a catacomb of little cramped rooms. The architects stained rather than painted the floors so that the original floorboards could be seen, keeping another memory of the past alive. And although an entirely new level was created in the basement, the original stairs were retained throughout the house.

As a way to further link the past of the house with that of its current owner, SITE decided to install actual objects that somehow relate to her distant or recent past in some of the walls. In SITE's conception, the walls act as a skin, a delicate membrane that separates and links the past and the present. If the skin is broken, the past and present meet. Mallet was closely involved in the choice of objects. "It is elegant humor, really," says Mallet of the riding clothes and classical mirror embedded in the walls of her hallway. "I've always been fascinated by horseback riding—what people wore—by this part of French society. It is a joke about how the establishment dress themselves and their houses." Sky sees it differently. "Those objects might have already been in the house—we know the original owners were European. They represent the past of the house, the past of the owner, and a projected history. The objects are about the questions they make us ask. We opened a wall and left a memory."

Both Sky and Mallet agree that the atmosphere of the house, the "special quality of intimacy" that Mallet talks about, and the "historical duality" that Sky imagines, is real, and palpable to almost everyone who walks in the door. "From the mailman to my children's friends to really sophisticated visitors," says Mallet, "it is accessible to everyone." She recollects an emotional moment in the building of the house when a wall was broken through and an old and tattered turn-of-the-century photograph of a woman fell to the floor. No one has been able to discover who the woman in the portrait was or why her photograph was buried in the wall plane, but the fact of her existence seems to reinforce SITE's conception of a design which so succinctly links the elusive past to the present.

Left: The floor and the door frame in the living room are original to the house. The bookshelves have books embedded in the walls as well as on the shelves, some covered with white dust jackets and some unjacketed. Mallet sees the bookshelf as "a joke about people who buy books by the yard" as a decorating device. The chair is the Proust chair by Alessandro Mendini of Studio Alchymia. The clock on the mantel is also an actual object embedded in the wall.

Left: The statue in the garden is described by Mallet as "the perfect cliché." It was made from a borrowed cast of a classical statue. While renovating the garden, the architects found old bottles that appeared to belong to the original owners.

Right: The objects embedded in the wall of the hall were chosen after much debate between the architects and the owner. The owner liked the idea of riding gear because it related to French society and a way of life she was fascinated with. The table and mirror also reflect the tastes of a certain stratum of French society, especially the "disappearing" mirror that the owner says is "part of a joke about what the establishment lives with." The owner was concerned that the objects "be tough enough" and not reflect too feminine a viewpoint. The vase is by an East Village artist.

Right: A disappearing door stands next to the stairway, which is original to the house. The architects have surmised that the original owners of the house were craftspeople, since the houses on either side of Mallet's house were used as housing for artisans.

FRIEDMAN

Dan Friedman, a New York designer of furniture, graphics, art objects, and interiors, has a vision of "some great apocalyptic event that will transform the world we know." His apartment, which he describes as a "post-nuclear environment," on the fifteenth floor of a Greenwich Village building overlooking Washington Square, overflows with the creative expression of his concerns, which are mostly about the realities of life in New York. "How can we exist from day to day?" he asks me. "How do we survive with all the heavy stuff around us? I'm not just talking about a bomb going off. There's the ozone layer, and AIDS. We need our fantasies, and a sense of humor . . . some way to find positive in the negative."

Friedman's apartment, painted in Day-Glo greens and yellows, glows as if it were designed in the aftermath of nuclear fallout. The walls are covered with Friedman's assemblages, weird sculptures that involve layers of architectural forms patterned in optically distorted shapes and colors. Some of the assemblages are abstract, others representational. One includes a crushed soda can retrieved from a garbage pail and sprayed Day-Glo orange, an object that looks like a radioactive fish, a painted camera, and a large neon-green cockroach, all displayed within a decorative frame. In corners or leaning against a wall are painted freeform shapes—curved, jagged, striped, or dotted—that Friedman used to alter the simple architecture of his apartment, originally a rental in which renovation was prohibited by the lease. "We all live in boxes, in buildings with other anonymous neutral boxes. The challenge," he says, "is to design with personal expression in mind, without reverting to recipes from Bloomingdale's catalogues or style books." Friedman believes in designing with limited means, finding bits of furniture from trash bins and junk shops, and making new furniture out of parts of discarded chairs and sofas. He paints and repaints constantly as inspiration strikes him. His walls, he says, are like a diary of the past nine years, a mirror of his constantly changing moods and emotions. "A designer ultimately has very little impact on the environment," he reflects. "Riding the New York subway teaches you that. If we can't control the outside environment, we can at least have total control over our own."

Friedman talks with longing of a mythic world that he imagines will emerge from all the turmoil of daily life. In his fantasy we will return to the more mystical values of a primal society. The pieces in his apartment often feature grass skirts, decorative beads, and other simple fetish objects as part of the design. "The modernists misled us," Friedman believes, "when they told us form follows function. Form also follows fantasy. Someday the things we design will have spiritual value and cultural significance." One of the most striking pieces in Friedman's apartment is his Three Mile Island lamp, with a photograph of smoking "silos" on its shade and beaded trim, a piece which has sold around the world. Each time the lamp is turned on, its function is overshadowed by the reminder of a nuclear accident. A grim message about the horror of modern technology might not be everyone's choice of ways to light a room, but Friedman considers himself an optimist. "The message in my post-nuclear environment is really a gentle one," he says. "There may be an apocalypse, but with the right aesthetic choices, everything will turn out okay."

Right: The ceiling clock was found, as it appears now, in a street trash can. Friedman intentionally placed it on the ceiling to create a disorienting effect. The assemblage in the upper right-hand corner of the main room is called Krishna Corner, *made shortly after Friedman returned from a visit to India. The fountain to the left is called* Fountain of Youth, *made by Friedman in 1984. It is now in the collection of Angela Missoni. The green form is a freeform architectural element designed by Friedman as a way to alter interior space without reconstruction. The form can be placed anywhere in the room. The shelves at the back were found and painted orange by the artists L. A. II and Keith Haring. The devil sculpture is by the Brazilian artist Bruno Schmidt. The table was designed by Friedman.*

Right: The table in the foreground, located in the central room of Friedman's apartment, is his USA table, made in 1986. It is part of a series of tables that feature "trouble spots of the world." The screen at the left, also designed by Friedman, is now in the collection of Angela Missoni. The chair is a "customized" Corbusier chair with a fake fur seat and fetish decoration by Friedman.

Left: The plastic globes were part of an installation designed by Friedman that was shown with his "trouble spots of the world" tables. The bedspread is a "fun fur," the mirror a classical gilded frame from a Brooklyn flea market. The fabric light fixture was designed by Ingo Maurer. Friedman made the polkadot curtain. The chili pepper lights are from Mexico, and appeal to Friedman because he likes "objects that have a form different from their function."

Left: The assemblage is called Tornado Fetish, made by Friedman in 1986. To the left is a section of Friedman's Jiggle Figure, a totem made for an exhibition in Los Angeles. Friedman sees the assemblages as an integral part of the architecture, more part of the structure of a room than mere wall decoration.

W A R H O L

Right: Although Warhol
rarely had visitors at his
home, he occasionally used
the entrance hall for making telephone calls to
friends. In the left corner is
an early-twentieth-century
Italian bronze bust of a
man. The mahogany bu-
reau bookcase is George II,
circa 1740, and is signed
"Max Wilson, London."
The white marble bust to
its right is a nineteenth-
century portrait of a man.
The foreground bust is a
plaster portrait of Napo-
leon, attributed to Antonio
Canova, from the early
nineteenth century. The
classical carved gilt and
ebonized mahogany table
with a marble top is at-
tributed to Anthony Quer-
velle of Philadelphia, and
was made in the first part
of the nineteenth century.

When we arrived, the town house owned by the late Andy Warhol was in chaos. Boxes overflowed with plastic toys, Fiesta ware, costume jewelry, Art Deco silver, Navaho rugs, nineteenth-century bronzes, wigs, and clothing. Dozens of people from Sotheby's auction house, there to catalogue every one of Warhol's possessions for eventual sale, were wrapping paper around paintings and chairs. "I've just found another Rauschenberg," I heard one of them say. "Don't step on anything," someone shouts. A woman I never saw before grabbed my arm. "This is the biggest thing we've had in a long, long time," she told me.

It was late August when we photographed Warhol's five-story town house, almost six months to the day after his unexpected death. Until his death Warhol's house had never been photographed for any of the glamorous design magazines. He refused to allow it. "Andy never talked about what he had," we were told by Jed Johnson, Warhol's friend and the designer of the house. "He was embarrassed. He never used the house, never entertained. He would ask a taxi to stop a block away so that no one would see where he lived. His life, his real life, was out of the house." Warhol bought the Georgian-style town house on Manhattan's Upper East Side because, according to Johnson, he admired the architecture, which was very different from the converted firehouse he had previously lived in. "He liked the idea of owning it," says Johnson, "but did he really like the house? I don't know. Most rooms were never used. He spent his time in the kitchen and the bedroom. He was always waiting for a phone call."

Our plan was to make a record of the house as it was in the weeks before Warhol died. Johnson, who had lived in the house with Warhol for most of the seventies, worked with us to reconstruct, piece by piece, the formal, almost museum-like atmosphere that Warhol maintained. Johnson describes the rooms as experiments in decoration, from the formal parlor in the Federal style with its pair of nineteenth-century carved and gilded mahogany recamiers, to the jewel-like Art Deco sitting room and the guest bedroom one visitor called "the kind of room where Norman Bates's mother might have been comfortable." "Really, he just used the house to store his collection," says Johnson. "He didn't even like people to ring the doorbell." In the bedroom, where Warhol spent hours watching television and talking on the phone, his favorite pastimes while at home, a Rousseau hangs on the wall near the miniature nineteenth-century mahogany doll's bed that Warhol kept for Amos, one of his two dachshunds. Just before we photographed that room, something glinting on the carpet caught the light. "It's one of Andy's diamonds," Johnson told us with a wry smile. "He left them everywhere. He never knew where he put anything." A few of the regulars who used to hang out at the Factory were at the house, gloomily watching the Sotheby's crew at work. For the most part they ignored us—*House and Garden* had been there a week before, just after *Vanity Fair,* and they were bored with photographers. One of them finally wandered over. "Andy never looked at his work after he finished it," he told me. "Once it was completed, he put it in a closet. Then people from the magazines come in and photograph a *Mao* propped on his dresser with a bouquet of flowers." Johnson confirmed that Warhol never displayed his own work. As room after room emerged from the chaos, we never saw a piece of Warhol's original art.

As we left the bedroom, the team from Sotheby's was already pulling open dresser drawers. "Andy shopped every day of his life, but not for anyone to see," the young man from the Factory said. "He was private. The way he worked as a collector . . . he asked a friend if he should get any Venturi chairs. The friend said he didn't like them. Andy said, 'Will they be worth anything in twenty-five years?' The friend admitted they would. 'Then get two,' said Andy. That was how he did it."

Far left: Warhol's bedroom, where he spent most of his time while at home, was dominated by a Federal carved mahogany four-post tester bed. The painting at the left, from the early nineteenth century, is attributed to John Blunt. The lamp is a Tiffany favrile glass and bronze pomegranate lamp from the early twentieth century. The stenciling, a technique used throughout the house, was done by Jed Johnson, who experimented with reviving the nineteenth-century art of stenciling as wall decoration long before it became a popular idea in modern decorating circles. When Warhol was alive, the bedroom contained a large television set by the bed, stacked with video cassettes of old movies.

Left: In the corner of Warhol's bedroom is a Baltimore secretary, made in the early nineteenth century out of carved mahogany. The chest of drawers is one of a pair of carved and inlaid mahogany pieces made in Philadelphia about 1820. The carved and turned mahogany Federal armchair, one of a pair, is also early-nineteenth-century. The painting over the secretary is by Henri Rousseau. The miniature sleigh bed, made about 1840 in Philadelphia, was originally a doll's bed; it was used by Warhol as a bed for one of his dogs. The rubber toys on the doll's bed were part of the extensive toy collection Warhol acquired for his dachshunds.

Right: The parlor, designed by Jed Johnson, was virtually unused while Warhol was alive. In the room is a pair of classical carved and gilded mahogany recamiers made in the nineteenth century in Philadelphia. In the center of the room is a rare painted and stenciled brass-mounted slate-top table attributed to John Finlay of Baltimore, also from the nineteenth century. The table, originally one of a pair, was part of a set of nine pieces made by John Finlay for a prominent Baltimore shipping merchant. At the back of the room is a nineteenth-century carved, gilded, and inlaid mahogany secretary made in Philadelphia about 1820. In back at the right is an Egyptian Revival gilt and painted armchair from the early twentieth century. The figure forming the back is Nekhbet; the armrests are decorated with gilt masks of Hathor. The bronze figure of a young boy next to the secretary is by Paul Peterich, from the turn of the century. The Aubusson carpet is French, circa 1900. The portrait of the lady at the left is nineteenth-century.

Left: The walls of the fourth-floor guest bedroom are hand-stenciled. The painting is **Harem Scene** *by nineteenth-century French artist Georges Jules Victor Clairin. On the left of the center table is a late-nineteenth-century bronze figure of Mercury. Jed Johnson, who describes his work in the Warhol house as "experiments in decoration," looked extensively at historic houses before beginning to design any of the interiors.*

Left: The second-floor landing of the house has a console and two throne chairs from Warhol's collection of Pierre Legrain furniture made from galuchat and sycamore, circa 1917. The carved and gilded wall mirror is American, from the early part of the nineteenth century.

Right: In the Art Deco sitting room, above the amboyna and ivory chiffonier by Jacques-Emile Ruhlmann, circa 1933, is an early Roy Lichtenstein oil painting called Laughing Cat, completed in 1961. The pair of lacquer armchairs are by Jean Dunand, crafted in brushed velour about 1925, as is the lacquer and eggshell circular table. To the right is a galuchat cabinet, made by Pierre Legrain about 1920, part of Warhol's collection of Legrain furniture. The two spherical eggshell lacquer vases are French, made about 1925 by Jean Dunand, as are the small lacquer vases on the center table. The silver pieces are part of Warhol's extensive collection of the work of Jean Puiforcat, the famous French silversmith. The painting, by Man Ray, is called Feminine Painting and is dated 1954. The sculpture is Head of Venus, made in 1915 by Pierre-Auguste Renoir.

B A R C E L O N A

C A P O   M A T E U

Preceding pages: All the walls of the hallways in Casa Comelat are decorated with etched and painted scrollwork, no two of which are alike. The decorative reliefs are stucco—smaller versions of those found on the salon ceiling.

Right: Glazed pottery, designed by Valeri, lines the wall next to the interior stone steps leading to Capo Mateu's apartment.

Miguel Capo Mateu is the third generation of a Barcelona family to live in the Casa Comelat, the opulent Art Nouveau house in the center of Barcelona created by the architect Salvadore Valeri. Valeri, a contemporary although not a colleague of Antonio Gaudí, began work on the house in 1906, the same year his patrons, the Comelat family, declared bankruptcy. The project was taken over by their neighbor, Damian Mateu Bisa, the founder of the Hispano Suiza automobile company and the grandfather of the current owner, who raised seven daughters and a son in the house. Despite the passage of time and the turmoil and destruction of the Spanish Civil War, the Casa Comelat remains almost perfectly intact, with a history that mirrors many of the social upheavals of the past decades in Barcelona. With its ornate wood paneling and splendid stained-glass windows, walls encrusted with glazed pottery and sculpted stucco designs, the Casa Comelat survives as a monument to a vanished era of decorative luxury.

Capo Mateu makes no secret of his family's affluence in the period before the Civil War. The grand salon was created for his grandfather as a museum for an extensive collection of ancient Chinese art, although it is hard to picture effectively displaying elaborately adorned objects among the colorful glazed pillars and dozens of multicolored wall motifs. Capo Mateu still remembers large family dinners held in the salon among the five-hundred-year-old Chinese vases. The elevators, which have the original stained glass and Art Nouveau light fixtures on each floor, were among the first in Barcelona, a radical innovation by Valeri and his patron. During the Civil War, Capo Mateu (who speaks proudly of having the same silver coffee and tea service as did his family's friend Francisco Franco) fled with his family during the Loyalist occupation of Barcelona. The family took with them some of the more obvious trappings of their wealth, including the Baccarat lead crystal chandelier made especially for Capo Mateu's father, some ancient ivory pieces from China, and their Limoges dinner service. The Communists requisitioned the Casa Comelat for their propaganda headquarters for four years, obliterating Valeri's frivolous etchings in plaster with political posters and installing a mimeograph machine in the grand salon. At the end of the war, Capo Mateu's family returned to the Casa Comelat, employing the sons of the original Catalan craftsmen who had worked with Valeri to help restore its splendor.

Capo Mateu currently lives on one floor of the house, in a traditional Spanish interior evocative of the conservative values he respects. The emphasis is on religious art, especially from fifteenth- and sixteenth-century Spain; tapestries; furniture; and ancient Chinese objects. Going from the turn-of-the-century hallway, decorated with such innovation and whimsy by Valeri, into the somber interior of Capo Mateu's foyer, one realizes how radical the frivolous designs of Valeri must have seemed almost ninety years ago. In contrast to the free and unrestrained decoration of the house, the traditional interior of Capo Mateu's apartment seems like a relic from several centuries past. It is difficult to imagine that it was created years after Valeri's extraordinary design for the Casa Comelat. Valeri, unlike Gaudí, appears to have been more concerned with aesthetic pleasure than with solving architectural problems or exploring the realm of the spirit, but his ideas are modern in that they follow his own unconventional rules. Perhaps that is why Capo Mateu says that while he feels the salon, the most extreme of Valeri's creations, is "romantic," he finds it "a difficult room, not easy to live in." He temporarily rents the salon to a modeling agency, which holds classes and fashion shows there.

Right: Glazed pottery and stucco decorate the salon walls and ceiling, done by craftsmen following a Catalan tradition dating back two hundred years. The opulent relief work is made of gesso combined with stucco, some of which is thirty-five centimeters deep and almost indestructible. The stained-glass door, which leads into a smaller salon, is original, made by the Escuela Masana, as is the glass on each window.

Right: All floors of the Casa Comelat have elevators made of wood with the original stained glass made by the Escuela Masana. The stucco decoration was restored by the grandsons of the craftsmen who completed the originals. The lamp is also original to the house.

Far right: On the far left wall is a sixteenth-century retable of wood from the school of Valencia. The chairs are Castilian style, from the early eighteenth century, covered in petit point. At the center of the room is a hand-painted Louis XV portantina, *or carrier coach, bought by Capo Mateu's father. The tapestry at the back on the left is fifteenth-century Spanish. On the back table are several ivories from Capo Mateu's Chinese collection, each over five hundred years old. The retable on the back wall is sixteenth-century Spanish. One of the oldest pieces in the collection is a fourteenth-century figure of Saint Luke with an eagle, placed on the left of the back table. The table itself is Spanish, from the fifteenth century.*

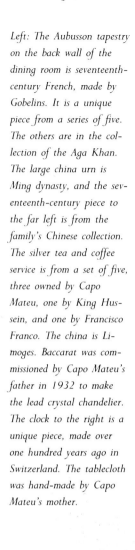

Left: The Aubusson tapestry on the back wall of the dining room is seventeenth-century French, made by Gobelins. It is a unique piece from a series of five. The others are in the collection of the Aga Khan. The large china urn is Ming dynasty, and the seventeenth-century piece to the far left is from the family's Chinese collection. The silver tea and coffee service is from a set of five, three owned by Capo Mateu, one by King Hussein, and one by Francisco Franco. The china is Limoges. Baccarat was commissioned by Capo Mateu's father in 1932 to make the lead crystal chandelier. The clock to the right is a unique piece, made over one hundred years ago in Switzerland. The tablecloth was hand-made by Capo Mateu's mother.

A M A T

Fernando Amat, the owner of a fashionable home furnishings store in the heart of Barcelona, lives in La Pedrera, the extraordinary anti-classical creation of the visionary Catalan architect Antonio Gaudí. La Pedrera (The Quarry) is the popular name for the Casa Milá, which was commissioned in 1906 as an ambitious design project for rental apartments by a businessman named Milá and his wife. The Casa Milá has been described at various times as "a mountain built by the hand of man," "a colossal architectural cliff with holes," and "an immoveable sea of stone." Amat, who had never been inside the Casa Milá before moving in, was drawn to the building by its strange appearance and by the fact that it was one of Gaudí's masterworks. "I would walk by it on the street," he says, "and I knew I could not live anywhere else."

As hard as it is to believe, Amat had very little competition for a home in the Casa Milá when he moved into a tiny space on the top floor in 1974. The Casa Milá, neglected and in sad disrepair, housed mostly small businesses, offices, and a school. Only six original apartments remained, occupied by longstanding residents. All the other apartments had been divided into minuscule spaces. Amat would wait ten years for a "real apartment" and several more before restoration would begin on the monumental building. Gaudí abandoned the Casa Milá before completion, frustrated by resistance to his ideas and by technical difficulties. He began the Casa Milá with the ambitious idea of creating an alternative to the traditional apartment building. His plan, to install a spiral staircase that wound around the inside walls of a courtyard to reach the living areas of the building and a ramp for reaching the basement for parking carriages and cars, was a precursor of the modern apartment complex. The facade was designed in disregard of conventional rules of composition, as a freeform, naturalistic "anti-facade," an attempt to blend architecture and nature. What began as a vision ahead of its time was finished as a conventional residential apartment by less ambitious colleagues of Gaudí's. Even Milá's wife, who apparently was not as enamored of the progressive ideas of Gaudí as her husband, completely redid their second-floor residence in the building in the classical style immediately upon her husband's death.

When Amat finally moved into his current apartment, he faced the difficult problem of designing an interior within a radical space that would not damage the integrity of the architecture and yet would reflect his own sensibilities. The walls had originally been painted in a floral pattern, probably by one of Gaudí's assistants, and were, according to Amat, "not very beautiful." After experimenting with a restrained palette of white and cream, he sought advice from the Parisian designer Philippe Starck, who suggested "Yves Klein blue" for the walls. The color is so strong, Amat says, that visitors are often intimidated by the sight of the undulating, freeform walls in such a vibrant hue. He decided to prepare them for the impact of the living room by painting the entrance corridor an equally vibrant green.

In visiting Amat's apartment, it is impossible not to feel moved by the scale and intensity of Gaudí's original conception, and also a bit sad about a work of great artistic merit that was abandoned before completion by its creator and then neglected for so many years. Structurally, Amat's apartment is pure Gaudí, with its flowing curved walls that defy conventional rules of proportion and design. Yet the moldings and detail work, done by assistants after Gaudí had departed, are consequently not as interesting as the decorative finishes in the rooms on lower floors. Visitors to Barcelona who flock to the Paseo de Gracia can peer through the grand freeform iron gates of La Pedrera into a courtyard in which traces of fading paint barely indicate the vivid coloration of the walls that once existed. Inside, one sees how badly the building is in need of the restoration that is now, apparently, finally in progress.

Right: The couch was designed by the Catalan designer Carlos Riart especially for Amat's apartment. The Gaudí taburete *(stool) is contemporary, made by the same company that produced the original, following identical techniques. Amat added an aluminum platform with wheels to prevent its being seen as a museum piece, "a Gaudí piece in a Gaudí house." The painting is by Angel Jové from his show at Amat's gallery, Sala Vinçon, in 1975. The small light on the table was purchased by Amat at a market in Morocco. The lamp table was designed by Luis Clotet of Studi Per and is of Arab inspiration. The door and glass are original to the building.*

Left: The ironwork balcony outside Amat's living room was designed by a student of Gaudí's, the architect José Mª Jujol. In a monograph on Gaudí, Salvador Tarrago describes Jujol, who collaborated with Gaudí on many projects, including the long ceramic-covered bench in Barcelona's Güell Park, as the most gifted of Gaudí's students in the sphere of plastic art. Tarrago writes: "[Jujol] created extraordinary collages which were ten years in advance of abstract and surrealist painting. It is inconceivable how, being far away from any contact with the experiments of the European vanguardists, both architects revealed a new world of shapes of such quality that sixty years later they have not been improved on."

Left: Gaudí designed all the apartments so that light would come in from two sides, the street and the courtyard. Thus, each of the inside doors has a glass panel to allow the light to pass through. The large chair is by the Barcelona artist Mariscal, a prototype for a show at the gallery run by Amat at his store. The painting on the floor is by Barcelona surrealist Angel Planells, a contemporary of Gaudí. Above it is a conceptual piece by the Barcelona artist Eulalia. The door and all the glass are original to the house.

Right: Details from the facade of Casa Milá.

CATERINA BORELLI

Right: The Catalan Gothic cloister surrounding a Mediterranean garden was part of a small convent for the Order of Clarissa, which was affiliated with the Santa Maria de Pedrales monastery. Franciscan monks lived in the monastery until 1835, acting as priests for the nuns of the conventet. *Eventually, the order sold the land to Archbishop Obispo, who restored the more decrepit parts of the monastery and the* conventet. *In 1918, they were sold to the first private owner, Angela Sorsy Darvin. A series of private owners followed, including the Battlló family, who also owned the renowned Gaudí house bearing their name. Godia purchased the* conventet *in 1968.*

G O D I A

Our first impression of the Godia house was of a grand building with iron gates and a hedge to block the view from the road, a typical house in an affluent residential neighborhood in Barcelona. The house appears new, with a columned portico leading to an elaborate foyer featuring a dramatic sweeping stair. Yet if one looks beyond the opulent foyer through sliding glass doors, one catches a glimpse of a garden, surrounded by old stone. Behind the new house lie the remnants of a *conventet,* or little convent, including an almost perfectly preserved Gothic cloister that dates back to fourteenth-century Spain.

Francisco Godia, a former race car driver, purchased the *conventet,* which was part of the Santa Maria de Pedrales monastery, as a home for his immense collection of medieval Spanish religious art and artifacts. The *conventet* had been owned privately since 1918, when it was sold by an archbishop who was using it as a summer residence. It first became vacant in the early nineteenth century, when the Franciscan monks who were priests to the convent fled Spain in one of the country's periodic bouts of religious persecution. The nuns returned later as the sole residents until they were forced to sell the *conventet* to the archbishop. When Godia bought the *conventet,* the gallery and cloister were intact, inspiring Godia and his architect, Francisco Folguera, to try to replicate the style of the old architecture in other parts of the house. The architect created arched panels that mimic the arches of the cloister and rooms with heavy Spanish-style wooden beams copying the substance, if not the spirit, of the original architecture of the period in which the *conventet* had been built. The result, a curious mixture of new materials and old design, is not altogether successful but admirably suits the museum-like display of artwork that Godia desired.

Godia began collecting as a young man, helping his father with the family collection of medieval religious art. Nowadays an entire wing of Godia's house is devoted solely to the collection, which is catalogued and cared for, written about and arranged by the full-time curator he employs. There is an embarrassment of riches on the walls in the gallery. A Picasso hangs near a fourteenth-century figure of the Virgin Mary. A fifteenth-century painting from the Flemish school can be found alongside a piece of Castilian sculpture. The collection is an eclectic mix of painting and sculpture from the fourteenth through the twentieth centuries, with an emphasis on Castilian sculpture dating back to the twelfth century. The walls are so densely covered with art and artifacts it becomes difficult to focus on any one object. To help sort out the details, Godia commissioned his curator to publish a monograph on the collection, and one on the cloister as well.

One has the impression that the cloister, to Godia, is another aspect of his ever-growing collection, purchased in much the same way as one buys an antique car or other relic from the past. It is separate from the main house in design as well as in style. The grandeur found inside the house, with its opulent dining room, ornate furniture, and extensive collection of valuable religious artifacts, is part of a modern statement about status and life-style. It is only in the cloister, filled with cypress, olive, and palm trees planted generations ago, that one senses the spirit of medieval Spain and experiences some of the tranquillity that must have been part of the lives of the women who first lived at the little convent.

Right: The cloister garden is planted with a variety of Mediterranean trees, including cypress, olive, palm, and bay trees. Beyond the arches, the walls are randomly decorated with antique Spanish tiles.

Left: The tiles inset into the walls are not original to the cloister, although they are authentic Spanish Gothic ceramic from the same period as the conventet. Each set of the tiles has a completely different pattern.

Below: The walls of the dining room display Godia's collection of Spanish ceramics that spans a period from the fourteenth century through the nineteenth century. The ceramics are from the regions of Aragon, Catalonia, and Valencia, including very valuable ceramics made in the small Valencian town of Manises. At the left is a fifteenth-century terra-cotta urn from Toledo. The urn in the back window is also from Toledo, made in the seventeenth century. The chairs are eighteenth-century Catalan from Majorca.

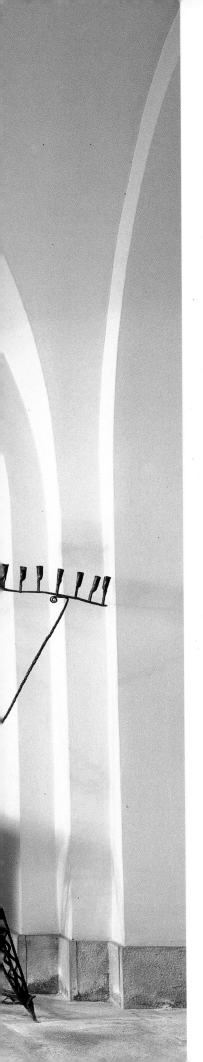

Left: The architect Francisco Folguera created an arched niche at the end of one of the corridors in the gallery as a display area. The large book is a cantoral, a volume of liturgical music, from the fifteenth century. On the back wall is a late-fifteenth-century Flemish school painting. The sculpture is Castilian. To the right is a lampadario, used for holding candles in a church, from the mid-fourteenth century. The Iberian ceramic bowl on the table dates from 1 B.C., before the Roman conquest.

Right: One of the most important pieces in Godia's collection is the painted limestone group representing Saint Anne, the Virgin Mary, and the infant Jesus. The piece, from Navarra, is dated circa 1300, and is very rare because of its large size and excellent condition. The chair is a monk's chair from sixteenth-century Spain. The dishes are Catalan, from the beginning of the eighteenth century. The drawing at the left is an early, pre-Paris Picasso, a portrait of Santiago Rusinol.

Right: Bofill found the location for his studio residence while working on Walden 7, a popular housing complex on the site of the former Sanson cement factory. The actual factory building, which now houses Bofill's personal residence as well as the Taller de Arquitectura, his studio, was purchased by Bofill in 1973 and remodeled in 1974. The project is unfinished, and is described by a colleague of Bofill's as "a permanent work-in-progress."

B   O   F   I   L   L

We arrived at La Fábrica, the factory that the architect Ricardo Bofill has converted into a home and studio in the industrial district of Barcelona, at night. It had rained earlier in the evening, and the wet concrete walkways gleamed with reflected light from the arched windows. The immense silos that form the core of the factory, dripping with inky-looking vegetation that climbs the rounded walls, loomed ominously as we groped in the dark looking for an entrance. The cement structure seemed like a sealed fortress. Huge rough-hewn wooden beams could be seen next to gracefully arched doorways. Curtains, unexpectedly placed outside near a garden, flapped in the wind. The effect, as if we had walked onto a stage, was disorienting. Although it was almost midnight when we arrived, one of Bofill's colleagues was still at his drafting table. We were invited to work as long as we liked, he told us—all night if we felt like it. Inside the building were narrow white corridors, like modern catacombs, leading up the steep winding stairs into the silos. Bofill has described the factory as "a freethinking lay convent with little difference between work time and free time. I have the impression," he writes, "that I am living within the walls of a closed universe, where the exterior—daily life—resembles Fassbinder's films."

Bofill found the former cement factory, which dates back to Barcelona's first industrial period in the late nineteenth century, over fifteen years ago. It was closed in 1971, but the silos, whose strange proportions seemed "magical" to Bofill, remained completely filled with cement and dust. Bofill felt that the factory, situated on top of a series of connected underground tunnels, was the embodiment of a new aesthetic, a conglomeration of aspects of surrealism, abstraction, and primitivism. He set about uncovering the essential structure, reworking spaces like "a sculptor when he begins to attack the material," cleaning cement and debris from the silos, and finally planting "a platform of greenery" as a base for the vegetation, which would eventually climb up the cement walls as well as hang from the roof.

The building is divided into three areas: the residence, where Bofill lives, a guest house, and the Taller de Arquitectura, Bofill's studio. In each area the architecture blends elements of industry, like the cement walls that have been allowed to remain, with architectural references to other periods, especially the Renaissance. The walls and the glass doors of Bofill's living room resemble a series of Gothic-style arches. The wall color, according to one of the architects at the studio, is also typical of the Renaissance. La Catedral is the name given to the terrace, where arched doorways and a vaulted ceiling are interrupted by protruding industrial shapes and enormous wooden beams. All detail and structural work on the factory was done by Catalan craftsmen, and many of the architectural elements, like the modern version of a Gothic window in Bofill's study and the Gaudí chairs in the living room, have Catalan origins.

There is an element of theatricality about La Fábrica, in part because of the drama inherent in a building of such massive proportions poised on the outskirts of a small, elegant city. La Fábrica seems a bit like a mammoth stage set, a factory masquerading as a fortress or a cathedral. Some of the drama comes from the contradiction of living and working in a structure intended for another, harsher purpose, of being in such close proximity to an alien environment. For Bofill this is a constant source of inspiration. "I continually have the impression of being in an industrial universe," he writes. "I live there now and work there better than anywhere else."

Left: Paint has been applied directly onto the cement walls of the living room. The only light is cast by bare incandescent tubes running vertically up the walls. The leather couches and marble tables were designed by Bofill in 1976 specifically for this room. The Gaudí chairs are reproductions by B.D., a Barcelona design company that has been reproducing Gaudí furniture since the 1960s.

Right: The indoor/outdoor terrace, which overlooks the garden, is called La Catedral, a reference to its high ceilings and arched windows. The space is used for concerts, dinners, parties, and sometimes job presentations that require large models. The surreal atmosphere created by the looming presence of protruding industrial forms is enhanced by a pair of flimsy curtains which frame the terrace as if it were a stage. The garden was designed by Bofill, who also designed the landscaping of the factory walls and roof.

Right: The window in the circular rest area, a room used by Bofill for relaxation and contemplation, is a modern version of a typical Catalan Gothic window. The bench is an original bentwood piece by Thonet. The radio on the floor is a reproduction of an early-model radio.

Left: The circular office for the Taller de Arquitectura is located in one of the silos where cement was stored when the factory was in use. The table was designed by Bofill for the studio. The chairs are new, copied from an original design by Thonet.

MILAN

GUERRIERO

Preceding pages: Guerriero painted his walls using spolvero, *a technique similar to stenciling involving shapes cut from paper. The flatware on the table is part of a continuing redesign project in which objects already designed are altered or embellished by another designer. In this case, Guerriero painted flatware originally designed by Castiglione with his own patterns and colors. The light at the right is called Papalina because its top looks like the skullcap worn by the Pope. The table clock is designed by Alessandro Mendini. The sculpture at the left is by Giorgio Gregori.*

Right: The bedspread on the narrow bed is a design of Mimmo Paladino. The bed was shown in the Verona exhibit called Casa per Giulietta.

"My apartment is no different from a monk's cell," Alessandro Guerriero says about the two rooms that he has painted in abstract pastel patterns reminiscent of the psychedelia of the 1960s. Guerriero, who founded Studio Alchymia, the Nuovo Design company, along with Alessandro Mendini and Ettore Sottsass, has a cerebral approach to design that is at once childlike and cynical. Decoration, he says, is like wearing makeup or a certain dress—merely a superficial way of communicating with the outside world. He believes a room can and should be changed as easily and casually as a sweater. His own walls are decorated as they are merely because he finds the colors soft and pleasing. The objects in the room do not have a function, and should not be expected to. "They are *oggetti dolci,*" he says—sweet objects, objects of love.

These simple thoughts about the aesthetics of living might be accepted at face value if they were not uttered by a man whose design company has been provoking controversy since its inception in 1979. Although it is true that most of the objects owned by Guerriero do not have a function, many have complex overtones and are designed as subtle comments on the contradictions of modern living. An example is the small figure of an animal that appears to be creeping up one of the pastel patterned walls. It looks at first glance as if a child made a cutout of silver paper and left it for Guerriero as a simple memento. The piece, entitled *Climbing,* is, in fact, a self-portrait by Alessandro Mendini. It represents the idea of "moving up," Guerriero says, of social climbing. Initially, the idea came from an Italian expression meaning "climbing on glass, doing something impossible," a wry comment on the outlook and approach of the Studio Alchymia designers. On Guerriero's desk is a Mendini ashtray shaped something like an oil can, which cannot actually hold a cigarette. If a cigarette is manually held in position at its tiny opening, the smoke comes out of the tall spout at the top. When I remark on its apparent uselessness as an ashtray, Guerriero smiles gently and agrees that it is impractical. Yes, he says, "it was designed as a way to quit smoking without violence. It is like a small factory."

Perhaps the most remarkable room in Guerriero's apartment is the small bedroom, also painted in abstract pastels, with a particularly vivid pattern on the door. Most of the space is taken up by a narrow bed and a startling wardrobe closet, which is mirrored and shaped like an upside-down U. The closet is the first object in what Guerriero describes as "a new phase of utilitarianism" by the Studio Alchymia designers. One can walk through the two "legs" of the U, store clothes in it, or see oneself in the mirror as one dresses. The effect of the piece, however, is dizzyingly decorative, since it reflects the patterned walls and makes it virtually impossible, once one is inside the room, to distinguish the real surface from the reflected one. The bed, which seems too high and narrow for a normal person to sleep comfortably on, was originally designed for an exhibit in Verona entitled *Casa per Giulietta* (Juliet's House), in which six teenage girls interpreted the role of Juliet on beds designed by Alessandro Mendini. This bed, a unique piece, is the bed of Giulietta's death.

Almost every surface or object in the apartment seems to be part of a design experiment. The walls, the blue desk chair, the tile mosaic on the terrace, even the motif on one of Guerriero's kitchen aprons is the same design applied to different materials, an ongoing project by Guerriero and Mendini. "This is how alphabets are born," says Guerriero. All communication, he believes, is merely a matter of aesthetics. A house is decorated in much the same way as a member of a certain African tribe might paint his skin. The skin becomes a filter between the spirit and the body, a superficial means of communication. For Guerriero, decoration is another of the many cosmetics of modern life.

Left: The sculpted vase was made by Lambert Escaler, a late-nineteenth-century artist who was a disciple of Antonio Gaudí. The foam flowers are the work of Piero Gilardi, an artist currently working in Turin who reconstructs natural forms in foam rubber.

Right: The Dipluro wardrobe, designed by Mendini, is painted with oils and has an insect motif. The Hispo table and the chairs are early Mendini designs.

Right: The Sirfo table and
Psilla armchair are both
designed by Alessandro
Mendini. On top of the
ready-made closet are a
teapot by Peter Shire and
a little chair entitled Sedia
Lassù by Alessandro Men-
dini. The Leopard rug was
designed by Guerriero.

Left: On the wall at the entrance to the main room is a fake barocco chest of drawers that belonged originally to Guerriero's family. The sculpture on the left side of the chest is by Guerriero. The vase on the right, called Vaso di Manici and designed by Alessandro Mendini, holds paper flowers made by Studio Alchymia to be given as gifts. At the far right of the picture is Climbing, *the Mendini self-portrait, which looks like a small silver paper cutout of an animal.*

Right: The papier-mâché Chinese clown in the entrance hall, from eighteenth-century Venice, has a bouncing head that is almost continually in motion. The walls are part relief, part trompe l'oeil. The obelisks and marble are trompe l'oeil. The seventeenth-century paint-ing is Genoese, entitled The Dinner of the Rich.

"The world is so big that it is hard to find something new," Renzo Mongiardino says from an armchair in the library of his Milan home. "The past is more of a discovery than the future." The library, like the other rooms here, is a triumph of trompe l'oeil, the trademark of this architect, interior and scenic designer, artist, and craftsman, who has been called the grand master of illusion. He is speaking to us in French, in English, in rapid Italian, ruminating about the essence of his work, the illusion of permanence, the link with artisans of the past, and the need to obliterate the distinction between modern and antique. As we speak, two men work across the hall in Mongiardino's small studio. They came to work with "Il Professore" when they were barely sixteen years old, and are now nearly fifty. Mongiardino considers himself a member of an ensemble. He remains committed to the ideal of the workshop, and to the *artigiano.* "They help me," he says of his craftsmen; "I help them. We help each other."

It is hard to reconcile the reality of this intense, modest, thoughtful, ironic man with the image of the famous designer who has created homes for the Rothschilds, the Agnellis, Stavros Niarchos, and assorted barons and princesses. His apartment, where he has lived for nearly thirty years, reflects a purity of vision combined with an irreverence for priceless objects that precisely mirrors the attitude of its owner. In Mongiardino's sanctuary of illusion and fantasy, the boundaries between real and fake, old and new, rich and poor are blurred beyond recognition and become unimportant. It amused him, Mongiardino tells me, to have an inside room that looks like an exterior Roman courtyard, so he put a seventeenth-century gilded bronze knocker on the inside rather than the outside of the lacquered wood door. The stone walls, the coffered ceiling, the marquetry, even the marble busts in the entrance hall are trompe l'oeil, executed with such skill that we find ourselves continually touching surfaces to determine if they are real or false. The seventeenth-century painting above the trompe l'oeil mantel is genuine, while the stool below is an exact copy made by Mongiardino from a photograph of the real piece in the collection at the Louvre. When I ask him how he chooses objects for a room, Mongiardino gives a shrug. "If a room is beautiful when empty, it will always be beautiful. If not, nothing will change it."

As a young architecture student, Mongiardino had a brief flirtation with modernism, especially with the work of Le Corbusier. He came to believe that modern architecture had too many limitations, that it was ultimately a dead end. After architecture school he designed sets for La Scala, where he began a lifelong appreciation for craftsmanship passed from generation to generation and developed the expertise about provenance for which he is renowned. "Houses have always existed," says Mongiardino. "A chair is a chair. We sit the same way we always have. Fantasy is in the many, many variations of the same things."

A delicate balance between idealizing the past and gently mocking it is characteristic of all Mon-giardino's work. In a small guest room in his Milan apartment, Mongiardino has recreated a scaled-down version of the room in which he was born, in Genoa. The furniture had been handed down through several generations, and when his mother died Mongiardino did not want to leave the room behind. The walls were given the patina of age by soaking the fabric covering in tea before it was printed. A portrait of his mother as a young woman hangs behind the bed. His guests sleep in the actual bed in which he was born. For Mongiardino, the illusion of permanence that he takes such pains to create is a way to link us to the past. The previous generation, Mongiardino believes, has cut off the past, but this generation is re-establishing a link with tradition. "We talk of centuries that are dividing us, but they are just seconds in the history of the world," he says. "Ancestors are not a past to remember but a future to discover."

Right: The tiles in Mongiardino's studio are late-eighteenth-century to mid-nineteenth-century samples from Naples, which Mongiardino collects and reproduces. The hand-colored prints are French drawings of upholstery samples from the mid-nineteenth century.

Far right: The illusion of being in an outside court-yard looking through the arch to the inside apart-ment is enhanced by the placement of the door knocker on the inside of the front door rather than on the outside. The wall and floor are intentionally damaged to further the illusion of antiquity. Through the arch one looks into the studio. On the back wall is part of Mon-giardino's extensive collec-tion of alterini, *small altars hand-made by nuns that Mongiardino began to collect thirty years ago. He first discovered them in Naples and is fascinated by the intricate architectural detail of each unique piece.*

Right: The furniture in the guest bedroom, a re-creation of the room in which Mongiardino was born, is nineteenth-century Italian, inherited from Mongiardino's grandfather. On the dresser is a little cup with Mongiardino's portrait on it, painted by his lifelong friend Lila de Nobili. The painting of Mongiardino's mother was done in 1913, the year of her marriage.

Left: The large library is a conversion of two smaller rooms. The wood, which appears to be nineteenth-century, is actually trompe l'oeil, as is the elaborate molding. The lamps, the globe, and the pool table are genuine nineteenth-century pieces. The back wall contains several more alterini *from Mongiardino's collection. The image of the man in front of the fireplace is an ad for a store that sells trunks. The painted panels were originally doors that Mongiardino found in Lombardy.*

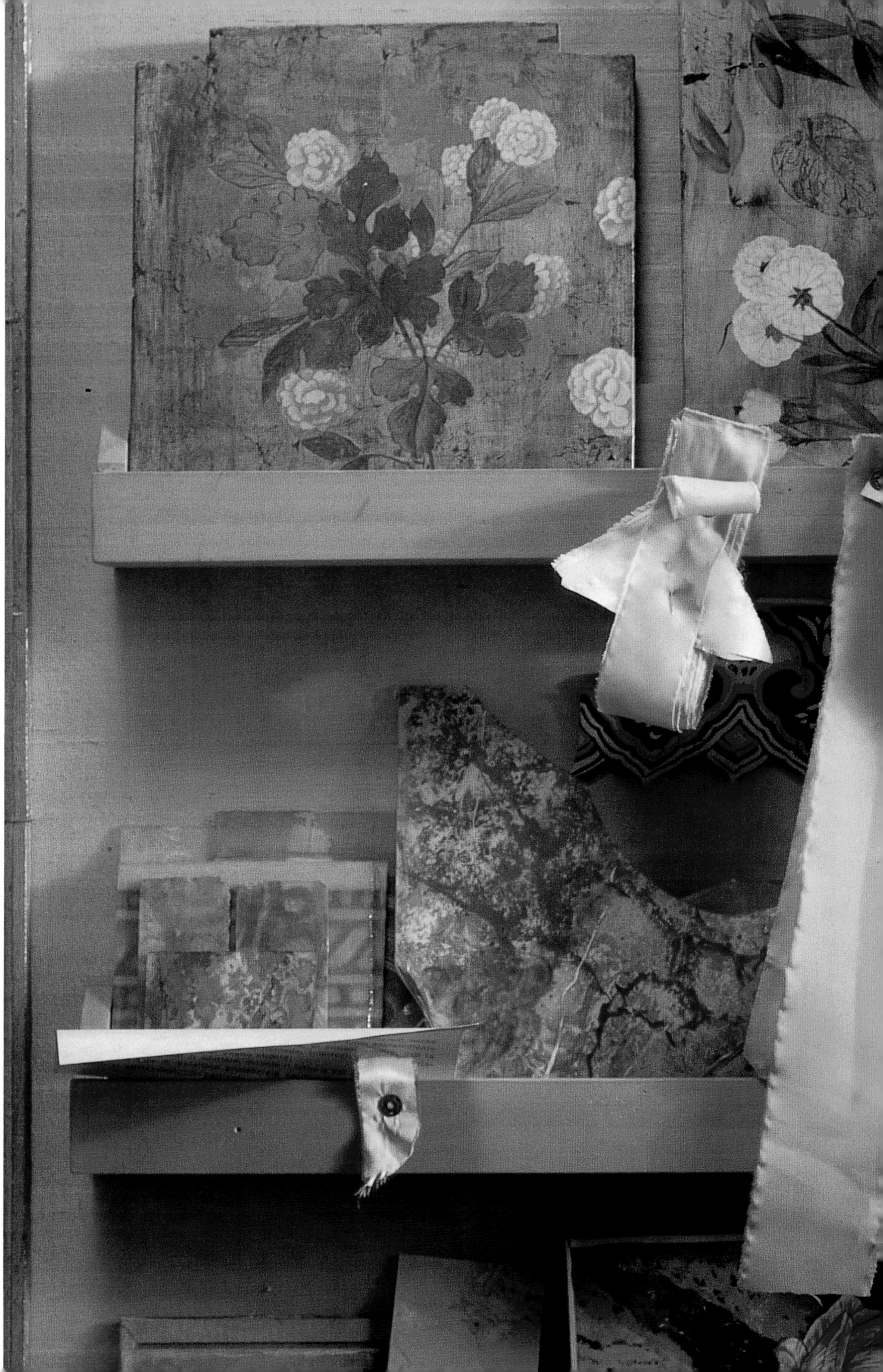

Left: Hand-painted glass
tile fragments and sketches
in a corner of Mongiar-
dino's studio.

Right: The sculpture in the center of the living room is eighteenth-century Indonesian, entitled The Wrestler. *The "pagoda" lamps are designed by Armani. The modern glass bowls are Italian, made by Vanini.*

A R M A N I

On the ancient street where Giorgio Armani lives and works, beautiful tanned young men with sun-bleached hair and leggy young women in miniskirts cluster in groups, chatting about who is in town for the collections. Outside Armani's door, we see a steady stream of male models, mostly Americans on "go-sees," hoping to be chosen for this week's fashion show (Armani's latest menswear collection). Armani's home and his offices are located in the same building as his showroom, which looks like a high-tech Roman coliseum complete with video screens, stereo systems, disco lights, and two sleek runways. The tension is palpable in the activity around us. Phones ring constantly, chic women in this season's black-on-black fashion uniform despair over seating plans, pinners, and pressers, and delivery men with garment bags rush through the huge glass and metal doors which stand out amid the old wooden and stone facades on the street.

It seems obvious that Armani has designed his home, located several floors above the creative chaos of his showroom, as a retreat from the hectic activity below. The rooms are spare and subdued, with very few visual distractions. The soft, cream-colored walls are made even more muted by the diffuse light cast by Japanese-style lamps designed by Armani. Furniture is minimal, and very low to the ground. No vibrant colors or decorative paintings detract from the peaceful mood. One's eye wanders naturally to the only color, created by the view of a wild garden seen through an entire wall of floor-to-ceiling windows—the single uncontrolled element in the apartment's design scheme. The silence, which we notice at once, is by design, to enforce the feeling of isolation from the real world. Even the walls and doors of the kitchen area have been constructed to prevent noise or the bustle of kitchen activity from penetrating any part of the apartment. In the traditional Italian manner, Armani always eats lunch at home, served by uniformed staff punctually at one o'clock, before returning downstairs to the business day.

This apartment differs from the minimalist apartments we have seen elsewhere. Armani seems to be seeking tranquillity in his daily existence through control rather than simplicity. Although spare, the rooms are decorative in that the textural harmony of fabric, the attention paid to color (however restrained), as well as the elegant placement of flawless objects are essential to the mood of the rooms. At one point during the day we spent in the apartment, a couple of newborn kittens began to romp on one of the low tables placed around Armani's living room. Suddenly there were two wriggling bodies, wild elements in a rigidly organized environment. The careful design scheme seemed to fall apart almost before our eyes. When the kittens were removed, the exquisite perfection of the room reappeared. "More than minimum decor," Armani has told me, "I find that cleanliness of line, the precision of the rectangular and square forms, are very soothing after a chaotic day's work." Precision is the key word here, because in Armani's elegant formalist home, even the slightest readjustment of a pillow or an arrangement of flowers becomes a jarringly uncomfortable, disruptive element.

Right: The wooden horse, the sole object in Armani's hall, is English, a gift from Armani's sister.

Left: The bedroom, like the rest of the apartment, was designed by Armani. Although Armani says he has not consciously been influenced by Japanese design, he has written that "subconsciously, essential elements of Japanese design have always had a great influence on my aesthetic taste."

B E L L I N I

A cobblestone courtyard leads the way to Mario Bellini's nineteenth-century palazzo, located in the heart of Milan. Bellini, one of Italy's most renowned industrial and furniture designers, is also an architect, an art collector, and the editor-in-chief of *Domus,* the architecture and design magazine. His work is perhaps more recognizable than his name, since much of what we have come to associate with contemporary Italian design was created by Bellini in his almost thirty years as a designer. That the creator of such modern furniture classics as the steel and leather CAB chair and the pillowlike Bambole sofa would live in a house built before the twentieth century seemed surprising. We were actually startled to discover that Mario Bellini lived with and collected very little from the era in design history which he influenced so strongly.

Our introduction to Bellini came from Gae Aulenti, the architect whose radical design of the Musée d'Orsay in Paris caused an uproar in the art world. Aulenti, a longtime friend of Bellini, was responsible for some of the renovation of the palazzo, which has architectural elements from the seventeenth century, the nineteenth century, and the twentieth century. It was difficult to pin Bellini down about which parts of the house he created and which were the work of Aulenti. "Let us say," he told me with a smile, "that it was a collaboration." To anyone familiar with Aulenti's work, her influence seems apparent in the divided stairway which separates the entrance from the main living area and in the elevated, exposed-wood-and-metal crosswalks leading to the library and to the dining area. The stairs are in two sections with a connecting platform at the top, which Bellini uses as a passageway and also as a display area for part of his collection of important sculpture from the 1920s and 1930s. As one walks from the somber arched studio with its red and green hand-painted murals toward the stairs, one cannot help looking up, at the dramatic sculpted figure of a reclining nude silhouetted against the ornate late-neoclassical ceiling that dominates the grand, sunlit main room of the palazzo.

This central living area is the room in which elements of several centuries cohabit and which perhaps best illustrates the design sensibility of the palazzo. Although the palazzo dates back to the 1830s, it was restored a century later by an architect named Portaluppi, who re-created the murals, installed the Gothic fireplace, and refurbished the ceiling. Some of the tables and sofas here are modern designs by Bellini, but many of the pieces in the room are originals by Alvar Aalto and other designers from the period of Portaluppi's restoration. Bellini's extensive collection of Italian Realist painting, which decorates many of the walls of the main room and the foyer, also dates from the period between the two world wars.

As we worked in the beautiful rooms of Mario Bellini's palazzo, we could not help but try to puzzle out the choices made by a man who lives in a style so far removed from his own creative work. In some ways Bellini's home is traditional, in that the blending of styles and periods within an older, grand structure is characteristic of the best Italian design. It is certainly fascinating to see how Bellini's furniture designs blend into an environment rooted in another, more elaborate sensibility. Perhaps the key to the house is in the garden, which dates back to the seventeenth century. Portaluppi restored the pool in the thirties, and Bellini and Piero Porcinai restored the landscaping a few years ago. Yet in spite of the many generations of alteration and influence, the garden appears as perfect and tranquil as if it had never been disturbed.

Right: The curtains that
separate the sleeping area
from the bathing area are
from eighteenth-century
Afghanistan. They are
made of woven silk threads
that have been individually
dyed. The Madonna figure
is painted wood from the
sixteenth century. The
painting in the background
is entitled The Return,
made by Giuseppe Gorni in
1919. The marble in the
foreground is modern, from
Portugal. The lamp was
made by Tiffany.

Left: The bronze sculpture
that overlooks the main living area and a view of the
garden is entitled The
Lovers, made by Francesco
Messina in 1925.

Left: The reclining nude sculpture, called The Woman from Pisa, *was made by Arturo Martini, whom Bellini calls the "most important Italian sculptor of the 1930s," in 1928. The lamp is a Japanese paper lantern by Isamu Noguchi.*

Left: The foreground and center tables and the sofas in the living room are designed by Bellini for Cassina. On the left are an original table and armchair by Alvar Aalto. The lamp is Italian, from the twenties. The painting at the left is entitled Double Portrait with Sister, painted by Felice Casorati in 1924. The teapots are early-twentieth-century German.

Right: The garden statue dates back to the seventeenth century, as does the garden itself. The urn is turn-of-the-century German. The pool was restored in the thirties by Portaluppi.

MEXICO CITY

G I L A R D I

The Tacubaya section of Mexico City is not where you might expect to find the last great work of one of the world's master architects. We rode around the tiny streets in a cramped Volkswagen taxi with no front passenger seat, past brightly colored shacks with the paint peeling from the walls, past dingy fruit markets, broken-down cars, and dirty-faced children playing on the sidewalk. We were looking for the hot pink facade of the Gilardi house, built by the celebrated Luis Barragán. Rounding a corner, we found it— a blank wall, intentionally austere except for its color. The exterior of Barragán's final work is, by design, a modest and harmonious addition to a working-class neighborhood.

The internationally acclaimed Mexican architect Luis Barragán died last year at the age of eighty-six. Until he died, he also lived in Tacubaya, several blocks from the Gilardi residence in an even less elegant part of the city. Before Barragán began the Gilardi house, he had not worked on another project for ten years. Francisco Gilardi had purchased a tract of land that came with a ramshackle house built in the 1920s, but had little idea of how to make it habitable. One night, over a few drinks, he and a friend began to fantasize about having the great Luis Barragán rebuild the house. On impulse, they called Barragán, who, to their surprise, agreed to meet them in a local cafeteria to talk about the project. At first, he told Gilardi, he might consider the project in three months' time. Then, he began to make some hasty sketches on a paper napkin. Soon Barragán was visiting the Gilardi house every day.

The emotional impact of the Gilardi house has to do, in part, with the contrast between the simple, formal structure of the architecture and the sensual, almost erotic use of texture and color. The hallway is white, except for the right wall and the vertical strips of window, which line that wall with the stiff formality of toy soldiers. The window wall as well as the windows have been painted yellow, throwing vivid color onto the other walls in the corridor as sunlight floods in. The space takes on a dreamy quality, intensified by one's inability to see out of the painted windows. At the end of the hallway is an almost mystical vanishing point of color, light, and water. The focal point of the house is the painted pool, the heart of Barragán's inspiration for Gilardi's home. Surrounded by a large, empty space intended for dining or resting, the pool is bisected by a freestanding red wall, which is reflected in the water along with the blue and white textured surface of the wall behind the pool. Once a day, in an enchanted moment, the unearthly interplay of color and reflection is pierced by a diagonal shaft of light, which becomes part of the reflected abstract pattern of color on the pool's surface. According to Gilardi, Barragán was unaware that the shaft of light, which appears to split in two as it hits the water, would strike the pool at all. "He painted the pool," says Gilardi with a grin, "and one day it was there."

The stories Gilardi tells about the rebuilding of his house make it clear that the process of watching Barragán work was almost as enriching as the end result. Barragán moved walls, changed the height of each floor, lowered ceilings, built enclosures. Months later, he would move a wall again, fractionally, for reasons only his own eye could see. He repainted the house four times, asking the Indians who worked in the house to tell him about colors from their native regions in Mexico. He even took notes on the hues of their clothing. Although Gilardi commissioned one of the most famous architects in the world to build his house, he is proud that it blends in unobtrusively with the others on his block. "Barragán didn't want the house to be noticed," Gilardi tells me. "He believed we don't have the right to be pretentious. He was a beautiful man," says Gilardi. "He taught me many things."

Preceding pages: The corridor, flooded with natural light passing through yellow-painted windows, is a luminous passageway, leading the visitor to the pool, the core of the Gilardi house. Although one is unable to see outside, the golden light makes one constantly aware of the warmth and power of the Mexican sun. Barragán had been strongly influenced in his use of light and color by the "naïve" paintings of Jesus "Churcho" Reyes, a folk artist and lifelong friend of Barragán's.

Right: Barragán's preference, which reflects his own modesty as well as his spiritual affinity with working people, was for an unremarkable facade. He did not want the houses he created to stand out from the others on the block. In this case, pink was chosen so that the house would blend with the other brilliant colors used by neighboring residents. The window is painted yellow to soften the light within and to prevent a view of the street from shattering the privacy of the room.

Far left: Water has always been a continual presence in Barragán's architecture. In the Gilardi pool one hardly knows which surface is solid and which is liquid. The sun softens and bisects the tactile surface of the blue wall, while the water acts as a mirror, reflecting light and color. The red wall appears weightless, seemingly floating in the water around it. There is a suggestion of mystery in the unseen region lurking behind the dazzling red wall. The shaft of light appears only on certain days for a few moments, in accordance with the earth's movement and position, and then disappears.

Left: A stairway without a rail, which seems to float in space, is characteristic of the architecture of Luis Barragán. An admirer of surrealism, Barragán often created a dreamlike environment in which structural essentials seem to be effortlessly supported in light and air. This unearthly quality is enhanced by the harsh, white sunlight that Barragán allowed to pour through open doors on each level of the house. When one looks out, or up the stairs, the view is shrouded and made mysterious, as the eye tries to adjust to the intense burning sunlight.

Right: The stone on the floor of the patio, cantera de aguascalientes, *is a material frequently used by Barragán. The stone is very soft, and even when the sun shines directly on it, one can walk across it in bare feet without getting burned. When wet, the surface is not slippery. The balls, made of a stone called* cantera dorada, *contain metal to keep them from rolling. They come from the Guadalajara region, the site of Barragán's native pueblo.*

Far left: The walled garden, or patio, a characteristic feature of most Mexican homes, was originally developed in response to the Mexican climate. In Barragán's architecture, the enclosed patio, created by the formal use of foreground, middle ground, and background, is a private place whose seclusion is seductive and mysterious. In his book The Architecture of Luis Barragán, *Emilio Ambasz has written: "Paint for [Barragán] is like a garment the wall puts on to relate to its surroundings." Here, the purple wall duplicates the color of the blossoms of the jacaranda tree, which bursts into color in the spring. The wall serves as a year-round reminder of the drama of nature, as well as a barrier against any intrusion into the serenity and solitude of the patio.*

Left: In another small enclosed patio, outside a bedroom, chimney pots for distilling mescal, a liquor similar to tequila, are the only objects. At one time they had been submerged in the pool at Luis Barragán's own home. He gave them to Gilardi as an unexpected gift several years after the Gilardi house had been completed.

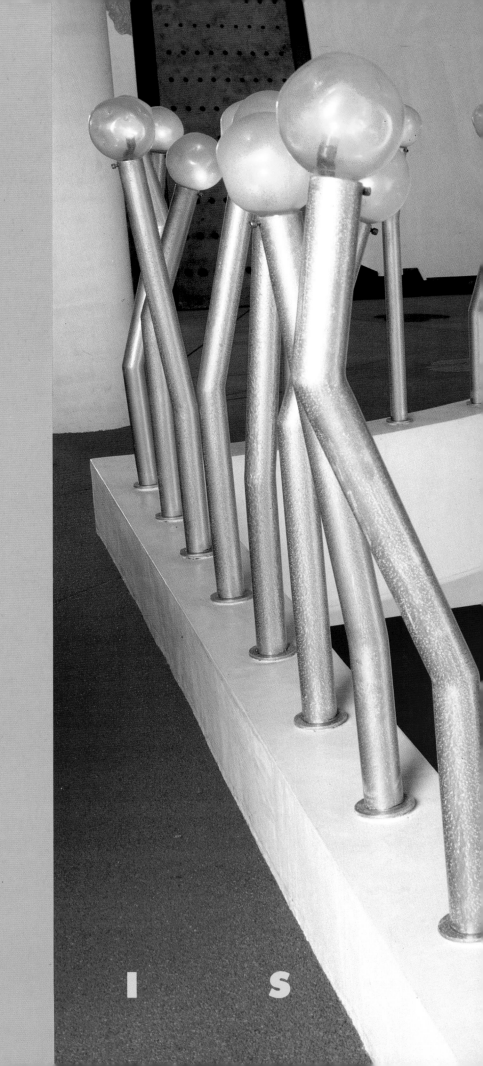

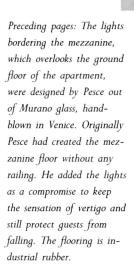

H U B I N

In the Parisian apartment created by the architect and designer Gaetano Pesce for his client Marc Hubin, a bed is wrapped like a brown paper parcel. Floor tiles are unexpectedly mirrored at random intervals. A door shaped like a hand stands only three feet high, forcing a visitor to crouch to enter the room beyond it. Walking on the mezzanine level, one is protected from falling over the edge only by narrow metal tubes with glass bulbs at the top, which seem to have sprouted along the border like avant-garde flowers. Slippery uncarpeted stairs have no hand rails. Chairs that look like soft, inviting shawls are actually hard, with strange sketches of unsmiling faces on some of them. "Like a city," says Gaetano Pesce, "the architecture within a home should always create surprise."

There is an exquisite logic behind Pesce's unique design for Hubin's apartment. "Function is important," he admits, "but if we can also express something, why not? Bed is always a surprise," he explains when asked about the hard shell which converts the bed in a guest bedroom into an anonymous package tied by rope. In bed, Pesce reasons, we never know what to expect. "Good dreams, bad dreams, no dreams, or will we sleep at all?" he asks. "And if someone else is there with us . . . more surprises. . . ." To Pesce, a wrapped and unmarked package, with no outside clue to its contents and no identifying decoration, symbolizes what we experience during the surprises of the night.

That Hubin's avant-garde apartment is located on one of the grandest, most conservative avenues on the Right Bank is an irony not lost on Pesce. The tricolor curtains on the windows of the huge living room were inspired by the proximity of the apartment to the Arc de Triomphe, which can be seen from an outside balcony. Pesce enjoys the relationship between the view and the architecture, and, as with every detail in the apartment, sees it as imbued with a meaning beyond the obvious. "We cannot just live with symbols," he insists. "A flag is important, but wouldn't it be better as something useful? Why not make a curtain out of it?" Pesce and Hubin recount with amusement that the curtain was seen by Paris soccer fans after a match one night when the painted fabric was hung outside the window to dry. The patriotic fans saw the curtain as a symbol of national pride, and soon a cheering crowd had gathered in front of Hubin's building.

Pesce worked with artisans in his native city of Venice to make the cabinets and doors for Hubin's apartment but he welcomed Hubin's participation, even in the craftsmanship. Hubin, who speaks of Pesce as though he were a brother, cut and installed the wooden moldings and painted the tricolor curtains. Pesce crafted and hand-painted the floor. Of Hubin he says, "He is still curious, which is rare today. The apartment is not mine but his, a fresh place, never boring." The last painting Pesce made in the apartment before its completion is a small airplane on the wall at the entrance. "It is a strange warrior symbol," he explains with a smile. "It represents a good fight, the give and take between the client and the designer." The real challenge for Pesce was to express something different and original in each design. "For me," he says, "a work of art is merely a useful object with meaning."

Preceding pages: The lights bordering the mezzanine, which overlooks the ground floor of the apartment, were designed by Pesce out of Murano glass, hand-blown in Venice. Originally Pesce had created the mezzanine floor without any railing. He added the lights as a compromise to keep the sensation of vertigo and still protect guests from falling. The flooring is industrial rubber.

Right: The master bedroom, seen from the mezzanine, has a circular bed placed precariously close to the edge of the room. The room can be sealed from view by mechanized aluminum doors that work like the doors of a garage. The clock is unique, a prototype for a smaller version by George Sowden. The portrait of Hubin, made by Pesce, was created by drawing on a liquid material that is then allowed to solidify. Pesce describes the process as "a fight with the material," because he must finish the drawing before it begins to harden.

Right: Shelves, screen, and chair are all Pesce designs. The wall painting is one of many unique tiny paintings found throughout the apartment, which, says Pesce, "create surprise and keep the architecture non-homogeneous, non-coherent."

Far right: All furniture in the apartment was designed by Gaetano Pesce. The chairs, made of resin and felt and bent by hand, were prototypes for Pesce's most recent furniture collection. Pesce used felt because "it has existed throughout civilization." The small table in the foreground is the prototype for Pesce's Samsone table, made by Cassina. The Egyptian head is from 500 B.C. The sideboard, faced with lead, and the light fixture are unique, designed by Pesce. The tricolor curtains are hand-painted by Hubin. The bedroom is visible through the back wall of the living room.

Right: The guest bedroom walls are zinc, "like Parisian roofs," according to Hubin. One enters the room through a very low doorway. The bed takes up most of the room, giving the illusion that someone managed to put a package, much too big to fit in the door, into the tiny room. The rigid "package" bedspread can be lifted mechanically, to become a canopy and reveal an ordinary bed underneath.

Far right: The door to the right, designed to look like a vault, leads to a filing area. To the left is the low door to the guest bedroom. The drawings, by Pesce, were originally inspired by Picasso.

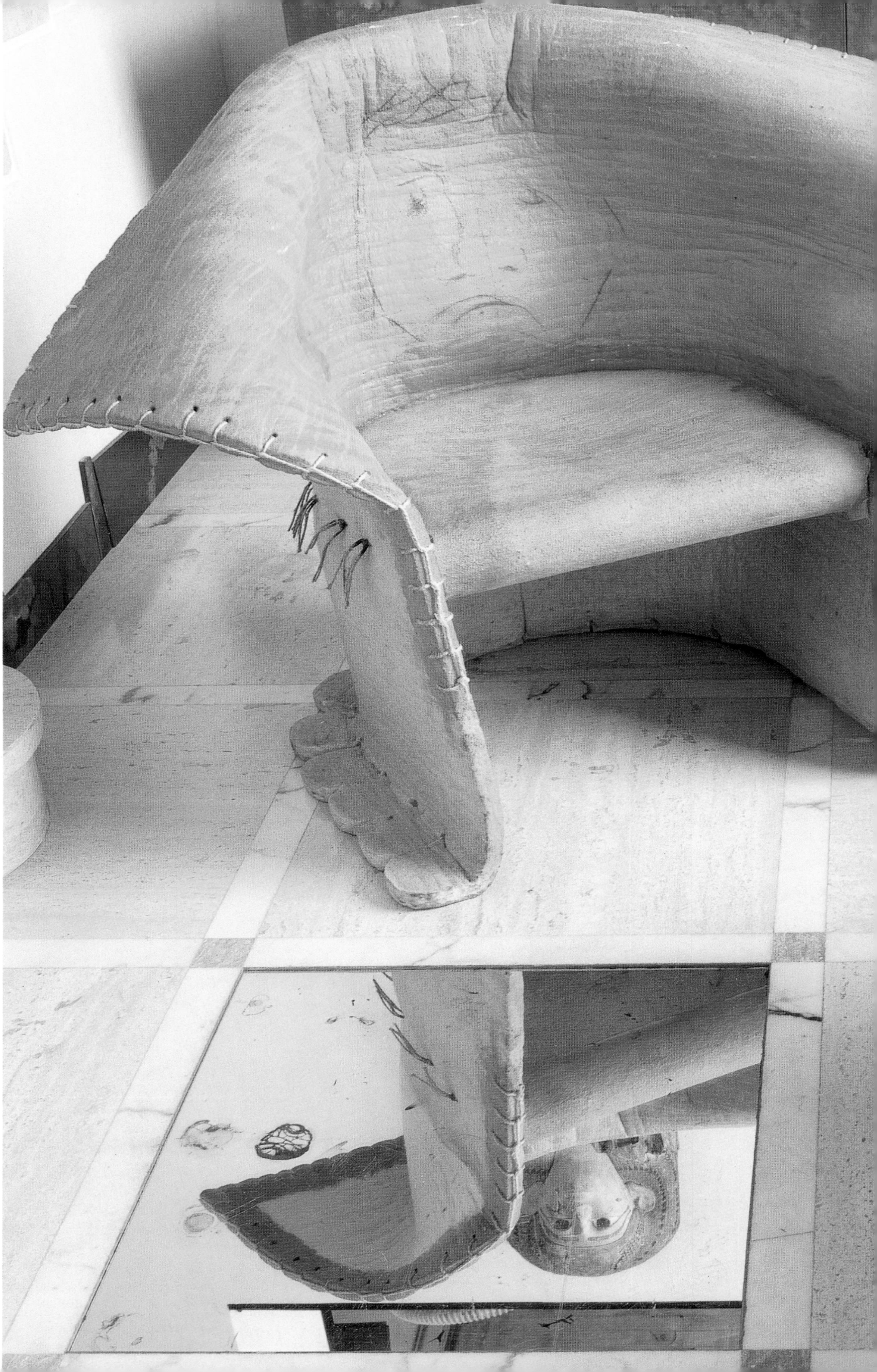

Left: The pink table is a
prototype for a series, each
one a unique piece designed
by Pesce. The protruding
rods are structural devices
also used as a design element. On the table are
prototype designs by Pesce
for Vittel water bottles. The
drawing on the prototype
chair is by Pesce. Now that
the chair is manufactured
in quantity, Pesce allows
the factory workers to make
original drawings on the
chairs, both as a method to
involve the workers in his
craft and to maintain the
originality of each piece.

V A L L O I S

In the rue de Seine, on the Left Bank, the Vallois live with their extraordinary collection of Art Deco in a rarefied atmosphere reminiscent of Paris in the 1920s. On the street, amid the art galleries, shops, and cafés, everyone seems to know Cheska and Bob Vallois. For seventeen years, the Galerie Vallois has been the definitive source in Paris for decorative art from the twenties and thirties. Yet few people know the intensely personal, private collection in the Vallois home, which is located across the street in a building that was once an old factory.

Less than twenty years ago, when the factory that would become their home was still manufacturing kitchen equipment, the Vallois began to collect Art Deco. It was a bold, unfashionable occupation during the 1960s and early 1970s, when students were rioting in the streets of Paris and one's politics were considered more important than one's possessions. In the ephemeral world of antiques, Art Deco had fallen out of fashion. It was a movement born of the careless extravagance of the 1920s. The creators of Art Deco, mainly painters and sculptors, revered beauty, opulence, and, most of all, luxury. They had been encouraged by wealthy patrons with money to burn to produce intentionally anti-functional art objects, such as fragile glass vases so slender that a single flower would cause them to topple, or chests of drawers too delicate to open. True Art Deco, as opposed to the kitsch Art Deco of the period, lasted as a movement only until the early thirties, when the international Depression made financial survival all but impossible for these impractical designers. By the 1960s, most knowledgeable people dismissed Art Deco as merely decorative, certainly not worth collecting seriously. The Vallois were able, through luck, timing, and a brazen disregard for conventional wisdom, to amass a personal collection like no other in the world.

For the visitor entering the Vallois home for the first time, the drama of the large interior sculpture garden is heightened by the gentle sound of water cascading down its walls. The idea for the garden was derived from the Japanese concept of bringing the more serene elements of nature into the home. The exceptional collection of objects, furniture, and sculpture is bathed in unearthly light from the skylight, which bisects the entire ground floor of the apartment. Seemingly unchanging, the consistent light, falling on the restrained palette of ivory, black, and gold in the walls and furniture, enhances the visitor's impression that time is standing still. Although the names in the Vallois collection—Jacques-Emile Ruhlmann, Gustave Miklos, Armand-Albert Rateau, Pierre Chareau, Joseph Czaky, Eileen Gray—read like a collector's guide, the Vallois insist that each piece has a meaning for them beyond commercial value. "We began with nothing," says Cheska Vallois. "What you see here is not everything we have, but everything we are."

Right: The collection on this table, designed by Eugene Printz, includes a silver vase with ebony macassar handles made by the Desny company for Coco Chanel in 1930. The silver platter was designed by Jean Puiforcat, the influential silversmith and sculptor. Arguably the most important French silver designer of the period, Puiforcat, whose inspiration was Plato, rejected surface decoration and deliberately created smooth areas that caught and refracted light. Jean Luce, a ceramicist who designed the tableware and glassware for the ocean liner Normandy, *created the four sand-blasted sculpted glass and gold-leaf vases in 1930. The bronze relief was made by Joseph Czaky in the early twenties; the alabaster and bronze light fixture is another by Ruhlmann from 1925.*

Left: *The hanging lamps in the corner of the Vallois living room were designed by Jean Perzel, an influential lighting designer of the period. The painting hanging on the parchment tile walls is an early work by the Russian painter Natalia Goncharova, made in 1913. The parchment tiles were made by stretching parchment over a square wooden armature, then clipping each square into place on the wall. The small eggshell-and-lacquer table is by Jean Dunand, lacquerer, painter, and designer, who pioneered the use of eggshell in lacquer and had a strong influence on other furniture designers of the period, such as Ruhlmann and Printz. Ruhlmann designed the armchairs on either side of the table in 1930. The stone sculpture in the foreground,* Seated Woman, *was made by Joseph Czaky in 1928.*

Right: An interior sculpture garden at the left of the entrance to the Vallois home faces the living room, which is filled with an extensive collection of Art Deco painting and sculpture. The sculpture in the foreground, The Accordionist, *was made by Chana Orloff in 1926. The torchères were designed by Armand-Albert Rateau, who decorated the famous apartment of Jeanne Lanvin in the 1920s. Pierre Chareau, an important architect of the thirties, designed the plant stand. Gustave Miklos created the gold animal sculpture for the couturier Jacques Doucet in 1927. The pedestal was created by Jacques-Emile Ruhlmann, the influential decorator who became known for stylized furniture using rare veneers or delicate inlays of ivory.*

D ' O R N A N O

Our introduction to the Count and Countess d'Ornano came from Henri Samuel, the distinguished Parisian interior designer, renowned for his expertise in French eighteenth-century decoration. His special skill, apart from having an exquisitely refined "eye," is adapting the important collections of his select clientele to the appropriate architecture. Samuel, who created the Wrightsman Galleries at the Metropolitan Museum of Art in New York, advised Countess d'Ornano on the decoration of this apartment. By her own admission, however, the Countess, who founded and runs the Sisley cosmetics company, was a client with strong opinions and decided ideas. The decoration that resulted was a collaborative effort, with the Countess's style influencing many of the design decisions.

Countess d'Ornano received us in the salon, an enormous ornate room with clouds painted on the ceiling and huge windows overlooking the Seine. In this room, as in the foyer, the walls, the ceiling, and the carpet are covered with seemingly unrelated decorative finishes and textures. "If you keep the harmony," the Countess insists, "everything can be mixed." She commissioned the cloud painting on the ceiling, which she describes as "a great element of decoration," and the mottled blue and cream walls against the objections of Samuel, but believes the results speak for themselves. "My first concern," she tells me, "is comfort. After all, we live here as a family. My children bring their friends here." Countess d'Ornano is an avid collector of Polish nineteenth-century painting, as well as royal artifacts from Poland and other countries, including vases that belonged to the Russian imperial family, an Adam table originally made for the British royal family, and porcelain figurines collected by Princess Radziwill, representing Polish court personalities. Some of the pieces of furniture and sculpture have an impressive history, like the chair in the salon that the Countess claims is from a group of chairs given by Napoleon to each of his field marshals.

The royal crest of the d'Ornano family can be seen on cushions and on the backs of several needlepoint chairs. Countess d'Ornano is reticent when asked about her family background, preferring that those details remain private. The late-eighteenth-century marble bust on the mantel in the salon, she tells me, represents a distinguished ancestor from Poland, as do several of the portraits in the salon and the dining room. The inspiration for the tentlike effect in the dining room was the Countess's memory of similar designs seen during childhood visits to the Royal Palace in Cracow. Whatever the inspiration, the d'Ornano apartment on the Right Bank, seen at twilight with river light softening the blue of the walls and glinting off gilded moldings, has been designed in the grand manner as an appropriate setting for a latter-day Countess and her family.

Left: The chandelier in the dining room is Crystal de la Granja, from eighteenth-century Spain. The wall fabric is a copy of an antique Oriental pattern. The Chinese vases are from the eighteenth century. The chairs and the buffet are early-eighteenth-century Regency. The armoire is Louis XV. The Saxe porcelain figures in the armoire were made by Kendler, described by Countess d'Ornano as "one of the best porcelain makers," and represent Polish court personages. The paintings are nineteenth-century Polish.

Right: In the far right corner of the salon is a sculpted silver statue of Henry IV similar to one found in the Louvre in Paris. The desk at the right is Louis XV. The clock on the mirror is also Louis XV. The rose-colored lamps were made from vases that belonged to the Russian imperial family. In the foreground, covering the table, is an embroidered antique Polish tablecloth. The decorative molding is eighteenth-century, imported from a château in Normandy.

M I T T E R R A N D

"President Mitterrand is definitely one of my best clients," says Philippe Starck, who describes himself as a designer of "buildings, luggage, sailboats, museums, theaters, flatware, and palaces." The assignment to design and furnish several rooms at the Elysée Palace came about as a result of a competition instigated by President Mitterrand as an egalitarian method for selecting new French designers to obliterate the opulent, elitist rooms previously decorated for Georges Pompidou. According to Starck, he submitted "a series of esoteric and incomprehensible drawings . . . just a few loose-leaf sheets based on signs and symbols" for consideration. That President Mitterrand was able to decipher these vague plans fills Starck with admiration. "He is extremely cultured, curious, intuitive, and decisive. The fact that he is President of the Republic did not influence the spirit of my work at all . . . it simply counterbalanced all of the natural suspicion which I feel for the interior decoration of private residences."

President Mitterrand's decision to replace the splendid interiors created for Pompidou was, to say the least, controversial, especially in conservative design circles in Paris already distressed by the avant-garde Centre Pompidou and the new museum for Impressionist painting housed in the renovated train station on the Quai d'Orsay. Starck admits that the rooms decorated for Pompidou, which were either moved to a château in the country or simply covered over, "were very creatively done, and to a very high standard," although not to his taste. As a result of the competition, all the rooms at the Elysée were redone in the modern style for the Mitterrands. Starck was assigned to do only President Mitterrand's office and, in the private residence, the bedroom of Madame Mitterrand. The choice of Starck, who has a reputation he does not discourage as the enfant terrible of French design, was especially controversial since Starck saw the many social and political possibilities inherent in the opportunity to decorate at the palace. "I would not do a palace for just anybody," says Starck, "as obviously the political resonance there is more important than elsewhere. It is bearable to design a palace with one hand, only on the condition that one brings the other to the service of the populace, and shares the benefits of working with the elite."

The design Starck eventually created for Madame Mitterrand's bedroom is certainly radical, but in aesthetic rather than political terms. The room is an austere white box, with a plain white bed looking not unlike a pallet except for a spare iron frame covered in white cloth. The surprising element is the ceiling, painted with a vivid mural that is lit by a fluorescent tube around its perimeter, flooding the already lurid colors in eerie light. "For the bedroom," says Starck, "I wanted to free myself from the classical bourgeois notion that paintings must be hung on walls. I wanted a more intimate interaction between the architecture and the painter's art, a sort of reflection of the unconscious." All the furniture was designed by Starck to have both a practical as well as a symbolic function, not unlike, he says, "a game of chess or a de Chirico painting." Although the materials for the room are industrial or everyday materials, a conscious design decision with political overtones, Starck's main interest seems to be in creating a room that would represent an idea—beyond its everyday function as a place to sleep. "This project set out to express the concept of a person whose spirit is assailed by uncontrollable images and thoughts. These images would be the ceiling. In all of my work at the Elysée," he says, "there is the notion of protecting him who lives there, not only from himself but from external and invisible aggression."

Left: The ceiling of Madame Mitterrand's bedroom was painted by Gerard Garouste, a close friend of Philippe Starck. Starck's conception was that the ceiling be "a poetic space, a link between architecture and painting." Starck has described his vision of the bedroom as a refuge within the palace where the owners could rest as they meditate on the painted images above them. He intentionally made all other elements in the room austere in contrast to the ceiling. Starck, who has described some of his furniture designs as "an acid critique of the French bourgeoisie," chose to cover all the furniture he designed for the Mitterrands in ordinary, inexpensive materials.

Right: The bed, designed by Starck, has a hidden circular tray, which swings out from underneath the mattress to act as a bedside table. On the wall behind the bed, a small alcove can be seen, designed as a storage unit. All lighting fixtures were custom-made by Starck.

Right: Rochline found this cardboard hand-painted desk in a local flea market. He believes it was used as a prop for a nineteenth-century French theater production. The embroidered fabric is antique, possibly eighteenth-century, another flea market discovery. The contemporary plaster figurines are part of Rochline's growing collection.

R O C H L I N E

"Why do I need money?" asks David Rochline. "If I want a marble floor, I can paint one. Tapestry? I can create one out of sackcloth."

Rochline is a singer, writer, performer, composer, set designer, set builder, and trompe l'oeil artist who lives in a factory converted into a castle. His aim is to follow what he calls "a recipe for the bizarre," which amounts to a personal manifesto about the impact of design on one's life. His intention in creating his home was to eliminate all signs of contemporary architecture, so that no reference points to the real world remain. No books are visible, no modern light fixtures, ordinary beds, closets, or bathrooms. To deceive the eye, he has lowered ceilings in some places, raised floors in others, so that the proportions of rooms are altered from what one might expect. "My ideal," says Rochline, "is to represent all types of architecture, big and small, in one place."

Aside from the skill of his execution, what strikes a visitor is the consistency of Rochline's vision. The three formative influences for Rochline—French nineteenth-century theater design, Italian Renaissance painting, and the films of Josef von Sternberg—are seemingly unrelated, but become a cohesive patchwork in Rochline's quirky view of design. He has always been fascinated by the power of illusion, especially as created by theatrical effect. As a boy he remembers seeing paintings of Nativity scenes in which the Virgin Mary was portrayed "as a Queen" although painted in an environment of basic poverty. Sternberg's *The Blue Angel,* in which the main character is deceived by theatrical effects into believing that an exotic woman is a goddess rather than a cabaret singer, also made a strong impression on Rochline. Initially, Rochline transformed his environment into a sumptuous theatrical set, in which he could walk behind the furniture, as if an actor on a stage. The illusion of grandeur which resulted alarmed Rochline to the extent that for several months he lived mainly in the kitchen. He solved the problem by painting broken stones and worn patches on his "castle" walls, and by adding props made from inexpensive materials throughout. The effect, he says, was to transform the illusion of a castle into the illusion of a simple farmhouse.

Rochline continually flirts with the juxtaposition of grandeur and simplicity, wealth and poverty, illusion and reality. His is an ironic approach to design and to life. One of Rochline's favorite possessions is a tea set that he guesses was made in the 1950s. He bought it in one of the countless flea markets he habitually canvasses around Paris, on the advice of an old tramp. "Of course I bought it," Rochline recounts gravely. "The tramp told me that he used to be a decorator."

Left: Rochline created this grand staircase out of paint, plywood, and cardboard. He painted doors that cannot be opened to give the illusion of additional exits and entrances to rooms which, in reality, do not exist. He enjoys a mixture of rich and poor elements as part of his overall design scheme. He painted worn brick patches on the stair to contrast with the beautiful (painted) marble floor. The plain wooden trunk is intended as a counterpoint to the more elegant urn in front of the staircase.

Right: In the hallway, Rochline has eliminated all signs of contemporary architecture, creating the illusion of a small, enclosed stone space. The balustrade is two-dimensional, made out of cardboard. The walls and the floor have been hand-painted by Rochline.

Left: Rochline's vision for the central room was to create a space where the outside and inside are merged. He hand-painted all the elements, from the outdoor backdrop to the sackcloth curtains and the sofa in the style of the great nineteenth-century French theaters. The table and chair are iron, made in the fifties by Gilbert Poillerat. The tea set, also from the fifties, is another flea market acquisition.

Right: The sculpture at the entrance to the Gastous' hallway is Utopia, *a one-of-a-kind piece created by Andrea Branzi in 1980 for Studio Alchymia. Branzi, who wrote about "the search for a new linguistic expressive quality as a possible solution to the enigma of design," was one of the founding members of Studio Alchymia. The Rigel glass bowl on the right was created by Marco Zanini for the 1982 Memphis collection. It rests on a hall table,* Structure Tremolo, *made by Ettore Sottsass in 1980, when he was still designing for Studio Alchymia. The table, which is no longer being produced, is part of the permanent collection of the Museum of Modern Art in New York. The mirror, called* Ultra Strawberry, *and the* Cometa *light are early Sottsass designs made in 1970. The model spaceship from the fifties was originally part of an amusement park merry-go-round ride.*

Entering the Gastous' nineteenth-century town house on the Right Bank, one has the illusion that modernism, the most influential design movement of the century since its inception at the Bauhaus in the 1920s, never happened.

Yves and his wife, Françoise, are antiques dealers who acquired their town house three years ago as a setting for their extensive collection of twentieth-century furniture and objects. The architecture was chosen as a protest against the hard-edged unornamented buildings that epitomize the modern style. At first one is startled, almost shocked, by the sight of these grand rooms, with their graceful nineteenth-century proportions, filled with furniture whose style derives from the iconography of the most frivolous periods of the twentieth century. The intended effect, a good-humored thumbing of the nose at convention, is emphasized by the non-traditional pale walls and the whimsical choice of pastel colors for the decorative moldings, a palette reminiscent of the 1960s. Yet the ornamental setting enhances the fanciful designs of the furniture and objects in ways that a spare, austere environment would not. Instead of appearing as isolated art objects within hard-edged, gallery-like walls, the New Wave pieces seem at home. The Gastous appear to have recognized an ironic similarity in the decorative roots of traditional nineteenth-century architecture and the new art furniture movement.

As a dealer, Gastou is something of an iconoclast. He has run the gamut of periods from Art Nouveau and Art Deco through the fifties, wrestling with the challenge of reviving unfashionable styles, then abandoning his quest as each revival becomes the latest trend. "I have always," he told me seriously, "wanted to defend what is indefensible." Then in 1978 he discovered Ettore Sottsass, the Milanese designer whom Gastou refers to as "the grand master of the end of the century" and "the Picasso of Design." Sottsass founded Studio Alchymia, a collective of designers and architects working in reaction to modernism, along with Andrea Branzi, Alessandro Guerriero, Michele de Lucchi, Alessandro Mendini, and Paola Navone, in the late seventies. In the service of Il Nuovo Design, Studio Alchymia produced unusually shaped objects whose function was not always obvious or important. The designers used unexpected materials like plastic laminates and colors that were intentionally ugly, bland, or garish. They wrote, with populist overtones, about a better world. The group proved to be financially impractical, but Gastou began collecting the work of Ettore Sottsass almost at once.

Gastou is, if not a visionary, an astute dealer. In 1981 a handful of Italian manufacturers became interested in Sottsass, who had just formed a new design group called Memphis with Marco Zanini and Aldo Cibic. (According to Richard Horn, the American writer credited with introducing Memphis in the United States, the name "Memphis" was inspired by Bob Dylan's "Stuck Inside of Mobile with the Memphis Blues Again," which was supposedly playing on a stereo in Milan the night the new design group took root.) The first Memphis collection caused an uproar in the design communities in Europe and America. Many of the best examples of Sottsass's work can be found in the Gastous' apartment, including rare pieces from his Pop-influenced work of the 1960s to his latest collection of gorgeously colored glass objects. "Every ten years," says Gastou, "Sottsass creates a work of genius."

Left: On the mantel in the living room, the Gastous have an example of Ettore Sottsass's work from the 1960s "Pop" period—the Asteroid mantel lights—as well as several pieces from his latest collection of glass objects. The Torso chairs were designed by Paolo Deganello for Cassina, and the sofa was designed by Paola Navone, another founding member of Studio Alchymia. Carlo Mollino, an architect and designer whom Gastou sees as a formative influence on the New Design movement, made the low table in 1948. The table holds one of Sottsass's most recent glass pieces, and a low bowl, also by Sottsass, called Arianna, made during the sixties. The rug, with its strange tufts of wool and metal rings, was created by Olivier Gagnère in 1985. The black sculpture of a seated figure in the corner of the room was created by Charles Cordier at the turn of the century. In the foreground is a prototype for a table by Michele de Lucchi for the premier Memphis collection in 1981. The statuette is German, circa 1900.

Above: Gaetano Pesce's Samsone table, made for Cassina in 1980, occupies most of the Gastous' dining room. The Pesce Delila chairs are made of molded resin. Shiro Kuramata, who designed the extraordinary Issey Miyake showroom in New York, designed the cabinet at the left for Memphis. The piece, whose black and pink colors are strikingly decorative, seems to be a shelving unit, although it looks a bit like a television set. Its true function is ambiguous: the inner shelves are small and narrow, and their placement makes them difficult to reach. The sterling silver centerpiece is Ettore Sottsass's Murmansk fruit bowl. On the marble mantelpiece is a collection of glass from the 1950s by Fausto Melotti, Archimede Seguso, and Dino Martens. The sculpture was made by Axel Cassel in 1986.

Right: The stained glass in the library dates back to Napoleon III. Shiro Kuramata created Side 2, a cabinet that Gastou calls "an homage to fertility and femininity," in 1970. Carlo Mollino designed the chair in the foreground in the 1950s. The console, called Tartar and designed by Ettore Sottsass, holds sculpture by Axel Cassel and Fausto Melotti, as well as a Sottsass glass bowl called Attitude.

Far right: The pearwood rolltop desk is a rare piece by Carlo Mollino made in Turin in 1949. Isola and Gabetti, Baroque-style architects working in the 1950s, made the leather and wood desk chair. The rug, also from the fifties, is French, by Patty and Mary. In the foreground, Shiro Kuramata created the terrazzo table embedded with fragments of colored glass for the 1982 Memphis collection. The sculpture, The Whirlpool, is by the turn-of-the-century French Symbolist Max Blondat.

Right: The silver collection was acquired by Nureyev on various trips. The collection consists of objects from "the zone between Turkey and Afghanistan," according to Carcano. Originally, Nureyev and Carcano had not thought of using the silver as a design element. "It came about of its own free will," says Carcano. "Nobody planned it, but it makes an exotic corner."

"I want to feel around me like a blind man, testing everything," wrote Rudolf Nureyev in his autobiography, published one year after his defection to the West, when he was twenty-three. He defected in 1961, at Le Bourget airport outside Paris, apparently on impulse. "There was something electric in the air," he wrote about Paris, the first Western capital he knew. "This really was a new sensation . . . the streets had the atmosphere of a perpetual party. I felt a physical attraction to the city." Yet he also writes about a feeling of nostalgia. "Paris looked gay . . . but [with] a hint of decadence, a lack of solid purpose." He arrived in Paris in June, without a suitcase, few friends, fifty francs, and no idea what the future would hold.

A quarter of a century later, Rudolf Nureyev returned to Paris as artistic director of the Paris Opera Ballet. His home in Paris, on the Left Bank (he has other homes in New York, London, and Virginia), overlooks the Seine and the Louvre. He collaborated on its design with Emilio Carcano, who studied and worked with Renzo Mongiardino, the great illusionist, in Milan. Together, Nureyev and Carcano created a sensualist's environment, a home which could only have been put together by and for a man whose passion is every aspect of artistic pleasure. Carcano says that his challenge was to find "the key to it all" to make essential choices among the eclectic items in Nureyev's extensive collection. "It was like," says Carcano, "creating a setting for precious jewels." The initial impression a visitor has, upon entering Nureyev's apartment, is of theatrical grandeur, a blend of exoticism and culture. One enters a small, sunlit foyer, hand-painted and gilded, with a black and white tile floor that has been transported from a castle in Bourgogne. Carcano describes the foyer as "a composite of everything, a taste of things to come." Inside, the rooms are like chiaroscuro paintings. Light from the river creates highlights and shadows on ancient fabric, leather walls, silver bracelets and boxes, marble and bronze sculpture. Huge lamps, converted from Florentine urns, cast pools of golden light into dark corners. The sensibility here is so exacting that there is no jarring element, and nothing has pride of place. In the salon, a wall of exceptional fourteenth- and fifteenth-century French and Flemish paintings emerges from the shadows, to be discovered only gradually rather than seen at once. The chiaroscuro effect is heightened by the light from enormous brass chandeliers, which have not been wired for electricity. In the evenings, the salon and dining room are illuminated by dozens of candles, like the great nineteenth-century theaters.

Yet the most striking aspect of Nureyev's home is the way the initial dramatic impression gives way to a feeling of intimacy with its owner. The man who, as a young dancer, wrote of his "compulsion to break out of the hard shell, to explore, to taste, to grope . . . to be able to work everywhere" is at the core of the extraordinary collections that define Rudolf Nureyev's environment. He is an impassioned collector who delves into the culture of whatever country he visits with the intensity evident in his dancing. Every piece in the apartment reflects an aspect of Nureyev's exploration of the world of music, art, theater, and dance. He collects kimonos from the famous nineteenth-century No theater, antique Turkish silver, French academic painting, khilims, and Chinese carpets. The hand-painted harpsichord in the salon has a stack of disheveled sheet music on its stand, since Nureyev plays it often. Margot Fonteyn writes with humor of having the young Nureyev stay with her and her husband, only to have him confess he was "dying" from not having heard music for four days. "Rudolf literally fed on music and he was like a starving man in the silence around him." His home in Paris is a visual expression of the many passions which are sustenance to this great artist.

*Left: The walls of the salon
are covered in antique Cor-
dova leather panels from
the late seventeenth cen-
tury, which Nureyev had
collected before moving into
his Paris apartment. The
sofas are covered in velour
de Genes, a composite of
smooth and glossy velvet
with decorative relief work.
The nineteenth-century
fabric, created using a
technique popularized in
sixteenth-century Genoa, is
from Nureyev's extensive
fabric collection. Carcano
supplemented the uphol-
stery with modern pieces of
fabric made to match the
antique fabric when more
material was needed. The
cushions are covered in
fabric from Nureyev's collection. The neo-Gothic
frieze along the ceiling was
made by Carcano out of
gilded wood and mirrors.
"We wanted to make a
Romantic* boiserie, *a period setting for the leather
to fix it in time," Carcano
says. The lamps, a collaborative design effort between
Nureyev and Carcano, were
created from late-nine-
teenth-century Florentine
urns found by Nureyev in
Italy. The shades are modern, made in France out of
copper. The Louis XIV mirror is another acquisition of
Nureyev's.*

Right: The hand-painted harpsichord is signed by Ruckers, arguably the most well-known harpischord maker in the world. Behind it can be seen examples of Nureyev's extensive collection of kimonos, some of which belonged to a nineteenth-century No theater company. The five fulllength windows in the salon are covered by patchwork draperies, modeled on a traditional style from the late eighteenth century. The fabric is part velvet and part antique fabric from Nureyev's collection. The antique armchair to the right is Moroccan, from the Regency period. The covers were made by Carcano using fabric from Nureyev's collection. Nureyev acquired the rare and important collection of early French and Flemish portraits himself.

Far right: An eighteenth-century Polish brass chandelier illuminates the room that Nureyev uses as a combined dining room and library. Carcano describes the nineteenth-century Empire table, made out of Vert des Pyrénées marble, as the "centerpiece of the apartment." The table, bought in Paris, was "not quite apt," so Carcano redecorated it by darkening the feet and reworking the gold trim. The Empire chairs are early-nineteenth-century Russian. Similar chairs, which are now rare, can be seen in the Hermitage in Leningrad. The magnificent draperies are eighteenth-century, by Gobelins.

Right: The inspiration for the entrance was a room once seen by Carcano at La Casita del Labrador, one of the residences of the king of Spain. The walls are faux bois, hand-painted by Irene Groudinsky, Carcano's wife, and several other painters. The chair, part of the set seen in the dining room, is early-nineteenth-century Russian. The black and white floor was transported, piece by piece, from a castle in Bourgogne.

A house, for Heiner Bastian, is an architectural setting for art. Furniture does not interest him; in fact, he feels it detracts from the most important elements of his environment—his extensive collection of the work of Joseph Beuys, Cy Twombly, Andy Warhol, and Anselm Kiefer. The word Bastian most often uses to describe the quality of life he aspires to is *austere*. When visitors to their stark white and marble villa in the Dahlem section of West Berlin remark on the cold atmosphere, the Bastians are gratified. That is precisely the intended effect. The emphasis of any house, Bastian feels, should at all times be on architecture and art, not on the unimportant necessities of one's private life.

According to Bastian, the villa has existed as it was meant to be only for a short period of time. Originally, it was owned by an upper-middle-class banker who had hired an architect named Ernst Lessing. The banker apparently had reservations about Lessing's grandiose ideas and considerably modified the scale and style of the project before the house was finally built in 1928. During the war, the house, located near the Dahlemer Dorfkirche, the Berlin church that was the center of anti-Nazi resistance, was used as a safe house for Jews, who were hidden on the upper floors. Although the house was not destroyed, some of the marble and most of the mirrors were damaged in bombing. After the war, the villa became a haphazardly cared-for boardinghouse, with the spacious rooms divided into cubicles and the skylights covered over, until it was acquired for the Brohan Collection of Art Nouveau and Art Deco and further modified to museum requirements. By the time the Bastians purchased the house in 1983, the villa bore little resemblance to its original incarnation, and almost none to the architect's ambitious initial conception.

Bastian and his wife, who both have a strong commitment to architectural restoration and preservation, began research that led, almost by chance, to the discovery of Lessing's original drawings. The villa, they decided, would be restored exactly as Lessing had intended, following the drawings, which Bastian describes as "astringent," to the letter. Many of the pillars, made of Deutsch Rot marble popular in the twenties and thirties but currently almost impossible to obtain, had to be replaced. The Bastians found an abandoned quarry and bought the marble in quantity, matching its color to the fragments that had survived the many transformations of the house. Rooms were restored to their original airy proportions, skylights were uncovered, damaged stucco was repaired, even the dining-room mirrors were replaced with eighteenth-century glass imported from England, matched to the pieces which survived from the twenties.

Since Bastian believes that the private life of a house is of little importance and should be reduced to a minimum, aside from a few inherited family pieces and a table to eat on, he has kept the rooms bare. The paintings are propped against walls rather than hung, since the Bastians want to ensure that they are the most important rather than merely decorative elements in each room. Even the "grand piano" that looks like the only major piece of furniture in the villa is really a sculpture by Joseph Beuys. The Bastians see themselves more as temporary caretakers of their house than as owners. "We just want to live with architecture and art," Bastian tells me. "Our private needs amount to very little."

Preceding pages: The entryway is adjacent to the main ground-floor room of the Bastian house and separated from it by marble columns. An untitled painting on the right wall by Cy Twombly, made in 1986, is the only object in the room.

Right: The sculpture by Joseph Beuys is entitled Memory of My Youth in the Mountains, *made in 1977. Behind it is the only existing self-portrait of Joseph Beuys, made in New York in 1979.*

ERINNERUNG AN MEINE JUGEND IM GEBIRGE

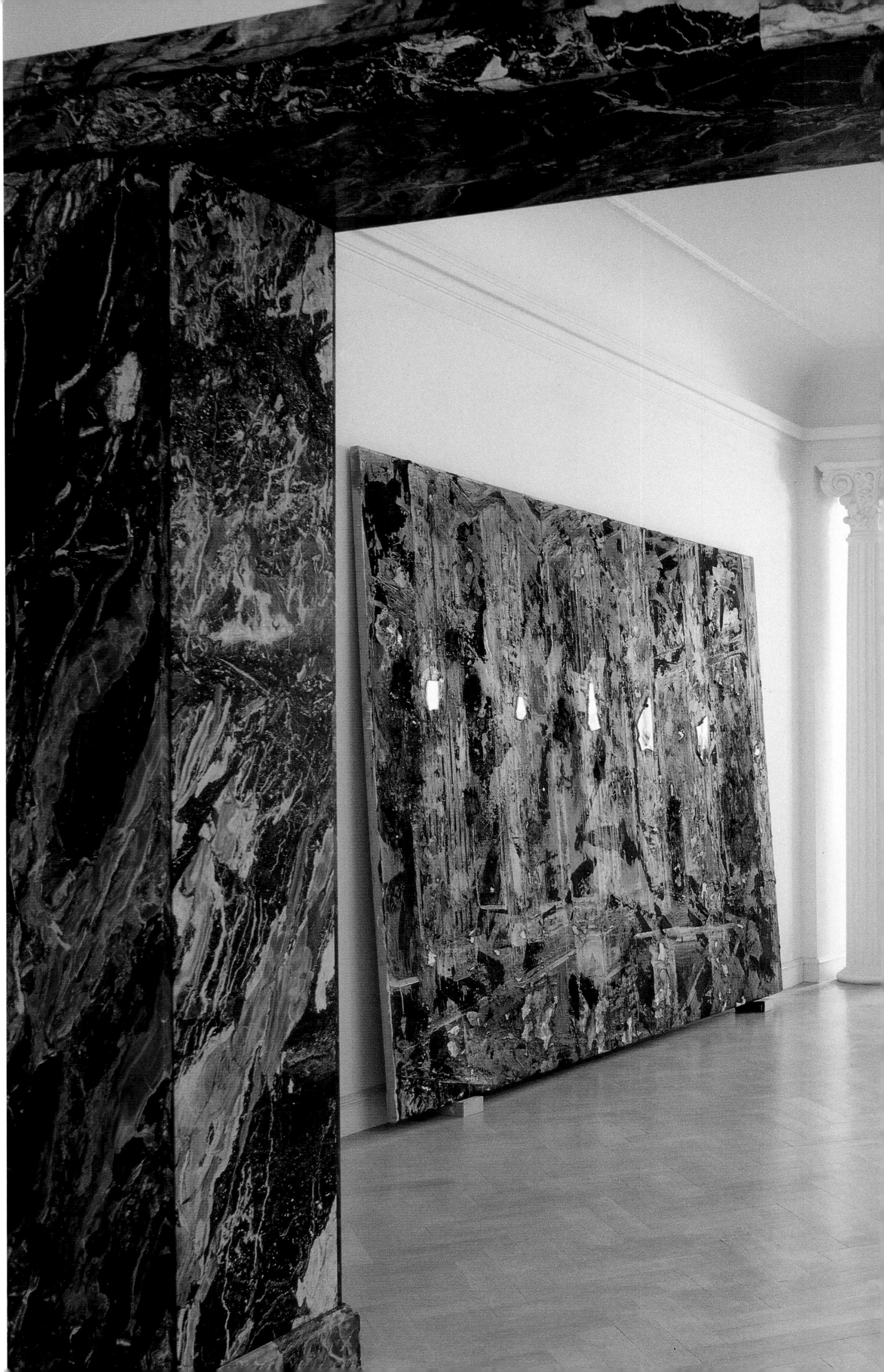

Left: The main room on the ground floor has French doors leading to the garden. The sculpture in the room, titled Piano, *is by Joseph Beuys, who began work on the piece in 1964 and completed it in 1982. A similar work by Beuys, covered with felt, is in the Centre Pompidou in Paris. Propped against the left wall is* The Five Foolish Virgins, *a painting by Anselm Kiefer made in 1983. Barely visible in the far corner is another Kiefer painting, entitled* The Painter's Atelier, *dated 1979.*

Right: This part of the house, adjacent to the dining area, also overlooks the garden. On the ledge are several pieces from Bastian's collection of antique toy cars.

Left: The mirrors, restored to match the originals, reflect the dining area. On the left is a first-century Roman bust of Aries, found in Asia Minor. The table and folding chairs are unadorned wood painted white.

*Right: Tobea Blumenschein,
a painter and set designer
who has worked extensively
with Rainer Fassbinder,
made these canvas self-
portrait curtains in 1986.*

W E I N A N D

White walls, bare wood floors, surfaces covered with avant-garde installations, and paintings by the West Berlin "wild ones," all "just put together somehow," make up the environment Herbert Weinand feels comfortable in. His apartment, located several floors up from the New Wave furniture gallery he owns, is typical of West Berlin housing of the turn of the century, with three adjacent rooms separated by sliding doors. Weinand prefers to live in older buildings, which are a rarity in West Berlin since the war, because he finds the high ceilings and square, substantial shapes of the rooms to be a good setting for his furniture collection. When I ask Weinand if he feels his apartment is *gemütlich,* the German word for "cozy," he roars with laughter. "No, I would not say that this is *gemütlich,*" he says, gesturing to the light fixtures he designed himself in the shape of nuclear missiles. "Chippendale furniture is *gemütlich,* not my home."

Wandering through Weinand's apartment is like taking a course in West German avant-garde design. Entering the narrow entrance hall, after climbing the inevitable five flights of stairs, one is immediately confronted by three looming gray rocklike forms that hang from the ceiling like threatening clouds. The forms are light fixtures, and upon close inspection one can see tiny lights imbedded in the gray matter at random intervals. The effect is ominous, especially because the massive gray forms look too heavy to remain suspended for very long. They make one think of falling rocks, industrial or nuclear fallout, or, at best, the sky before a particularly violent storm. The recurring themes of the art and objects in Weinand's apartment are typical of the creative work specific to Berlin, and stimulated by the circumstances of that city's existence—human beings threatened by atomic destruction, closed in by the Wall, haunted by the past. In one of the rooms, an emotionally charged painting by Salome, one of the young West Berlin "wild painters," shows a naked man falling headfirst into lurid colored flames. Tied to the ceiling of the same room with a rope is a Pershing light fixture, placed, according to Weinand, "at an angle, so as not to appear too hostile." Weinand has also designed Pershing tables, and, in another room, one can see his aluminum Phallus light, a moveable fixture with an aggressive shape similar to the "missile" light. The installation on the wall of that room might represent a human shape, a swastika, or perhaps both. The form is made from desk tops used in German classrooms in the sixties, when Weinand was a child and the Wall was erected.

The most striking characteristic of Weinand's apartment and of most of the interiors we saw in West Berlin is that almost nothing in these rooms is purely decorative. Even the most colorful objects, the most carefully realized and beautifully executed designs, are invested with a meaning outside their form or function. In Weinand's apartment, two of the windows are covered with turquoise curtains, painted with enormous figures of a woman. They are self-portraits by an artist whom Weinand says was a pioneer of underground painting in West Berlin. The two figures dominate the room. The eyes, like a surveillance apparatus, continuously stare down from near ceiling height. When outside light passes through the canvas, the painted faces seem to express changing moods. As with most of the creative work done in West Berlin, the boundaries between art and life are intentionally blurred. For Weinand, a designer, collector, and dealer in the avant-garde, this is as natural as turning on a light shaped like a nuclear missile.

Left: The wall installation, which includes the "sandwich" table, was made by the Hamburg artist Claudia Rahayel from pieces of school desks from the sixties. The Aerospace chair in front of it was designed in 1968 by Quasar-Khan. In the foreground is a piece of a plastic Zebra chaise longue, also made in the sixties, and a copy of the Manipulator *with a photograph of Ronald Reagan on the cover. The Fontana Art light fixture at the right is made by Castiglione.*

Right: The painting on the back wall, by Salome, is called Fallen Angel. *Salome is one of the Neue Wilde painters who founded the Galerie am Moritzplatz in 1977. Along with his teacher, K. H. Hodicke, and the painters Rainer Fetting, Helmut Middendorf, and Bernd Zimmer, Salome initiated a new era of emotionally charged painting in West Berlin. The photo on canvas by Wilhelm Moser is* Nuremberg Stadium, *taken in 1986. The Ball chair from the sixties was designed by Eero Aarinio. The Techno chair at the left was made in 1956 by Osvaldo Borsani. The red table next to it is Puffo, a prototype for Italian NO PARKING ZONE markers made in 1968. The tubular cocktail table has a ceramic top within a Michelin rubber tire.*

Right: The ceiling sculpture in the living room is titled Crash Lamp, *designed by two Englishmen, Lee Curtis and Tom Lynham, in 1981. On the wall is a painting by a performance group called the Deadly Doris, one of a series called* Strasse 1985.

B O R N G R A E B E R

Christian Borngraeber is an architectural historian and design theorist who lives in a sixth-floor walk-up in the Kreuzberg district of West Berlin. Almost no residential buildings in West Berlin have elevators, especially in Kreuzberg, a district of shrapnel-scarred tenements and stretches of barely habitable apartments adjoining the Wall. Tell any Berliner that Borngraeber lives in Kreuzberg and it will immediately make sense to him. It is a district of drama and tension, a neighborhood that in the late seventies began to attract a community of artists and performers who, because of its proximity to the Wall, saw it as a real and spiritual home. As often happens when a ghetto becomes an artists' community, living in Kreuzberg, near the artists, squatters, skinheads, and Turkish workers, has recently become chic. Property values have skyrocketed, and among the tenements one finds entire blocks brightly painted and completely refurbished. Borngraeber lives on Yorckstrasse, a tree-lined boulevard near several of the smart cafés that are beginning to appear. His Kreuzberg apartment, in elegant renovated housing that once belonged to a church, is some distance from the ghetto that still clings to the winding path of the Wall.

As soon as one enters Borngraeber's apartment, it is apparent that this is the home of someone whose intellectual concerns are art and design. In West Berlin design circles, Borngraeber is known as "the Pope," in recognition of his role as tireless champion, teacher, and leader of the new German design community that developed in West Berlin in the early eighties. A visitor to the apartment almost immediately looks up—at the twisted electrical conduit that has been made into light fixtures in the hallway, at the piece of sculpture on the ceiling of his living room, which looks as if a giant fist had smashed an opening in the plaster so that a light bulb could be dangled into the room. "Brutal and elegant" is the way Borngraeber would describe these objects, characteristics that he feels are part of almost all the new German design. Borngraeber designed the floor covering himself, using an old piece of ready-made carpet that he altered by pulling out threads at carefully spaced intervals. The idea, he says, was to "destroy the original at first glance. Then, with a second glance, you see the original." The walls of his apartment are white, as are the walls in all the Berlin apartments we visited. A friend told me that intellectuals in Berlin always keep their walls white, preferring to display the work of friends and associates than to decorate with wallpaper. Although Borngraeber certainly uses his walls to display his collection of art, he has painted a portion of each wall with a stippled gray wash, to create the impression of age or damage.

Destruction and brutality are the two concepts that figure most often in Borngraeber's discussions of new German design, and are certainly themes of the art and design of his own apartment. Borngraeber tells the story of one of the paintings he owns, which he says illustrates the "typical happenings off the Ku-damm." Two women, using the pseudonym Horst Reitz, created the large painting in one night. The next morning the two artists crept up to an elevated subway platform and hung their painting, a lurid depiction of a prone naked man held down by a woman's foot in a red high-heeled shoe, in a space normally reserved for advertising. Borngraeber, who had by chance wandered by, saw that the painting was about to be removed and destroyed, rescued it, and hung it in his apartment. The idea of the "Horst Reitz Action," according to Borngraeber, was to show the power and transient nature of advertising. West Berlin, Borngraeber says, is "a city of ideas." He believes that the new design often reflects the outlook of a generation facing up to the threat of nuclear destruction and that its creators live in an exposed and divided city. "Berliners," says Borngraeber, "are very tolerant. They have the time and ideas but not the money to create art and design. In the beginning, the happenings were typically underground. Now all the museums want the pieces."

Far left: The unique chairs in Borngraeber's living room were created by Siegfried Michail Syniuga, an artist from Düsseldorf, in 1984. They are titled Katholisch-Sunnitische and are meant to represent the cross and half-moon symbols of Christianity and Islam. In the background is a Biedermeier cupboard with a false front holding a collection of vases, including several Rosenthal and Hutschen pieces. The painting by Horst Reitz was made in July 1982.

Left: A crystal ball sits at all times on the cross chair. Borngraeber believes in the healing powers of crystal balls and uses this one, which he found by chance, to meditate with. The cushions, by the Deadly Doris, were used for a performance at the Kitchen in New York. The sofa, covered in cowhide, was designed by Borngraeber. The Brillo-pad cushion was made by Stiletto. The table, in plywood, Plexiglas, and rusted metal, is by Hermann Waldenberg, made in 1983. The piece in the background, by Piotr Nathan, a Polish artist, is part of an installation. The tripod is from East Berlin.

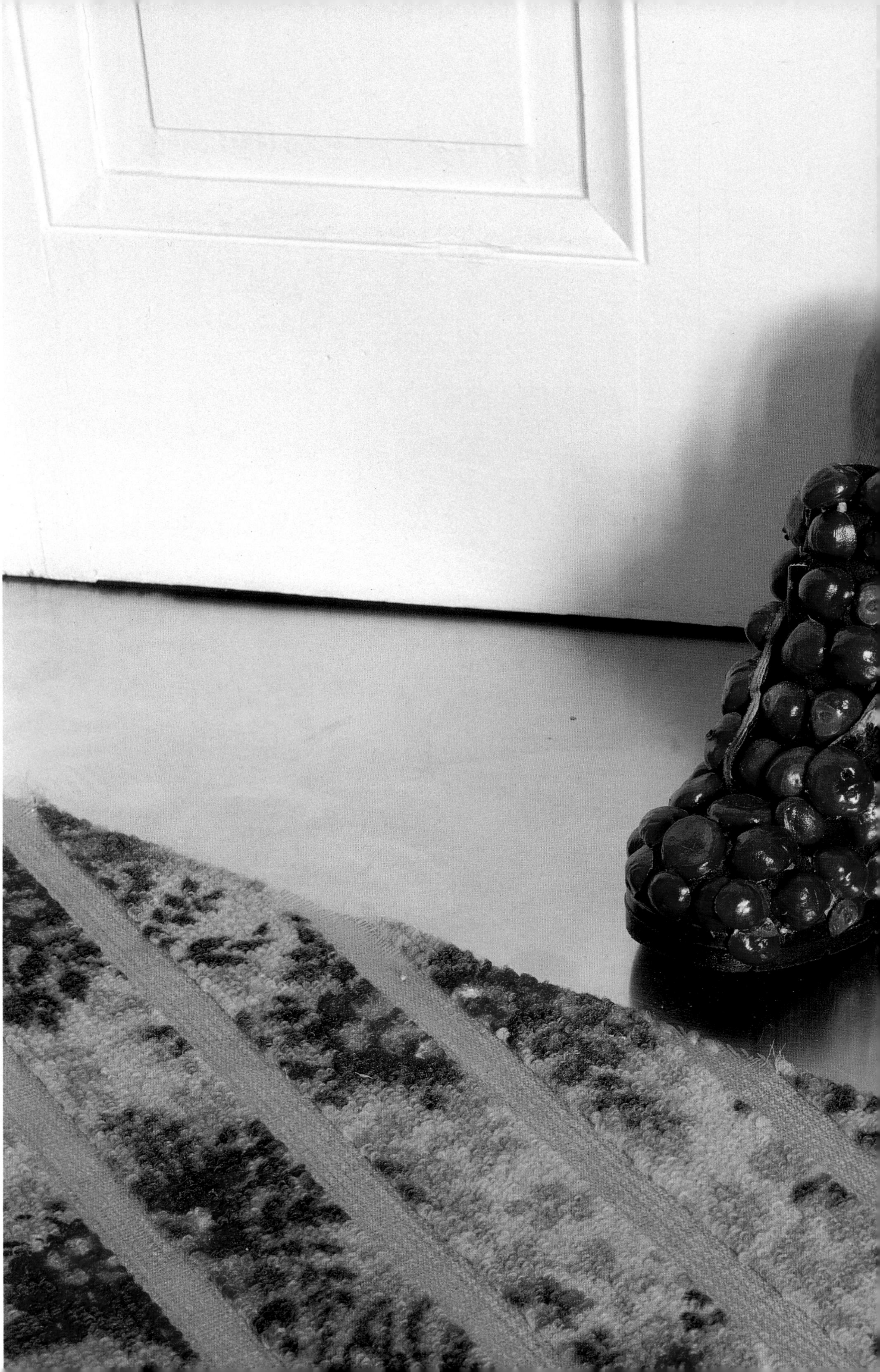

Left: The boots covered with chestnuts, designed by Ogar Graf to actually be worn, are considered by Borngraeber to be both artwork and footgear.

LONDON

N E V I L L

"This is not a serious room," Bernard Nevill tells me. "You realize, don't you, that this is not a final statement?"

Nevill is speaking about his drawing room/library in West House, the central room in his home in the Chelsea section of London. Located a few blocks from the Embankment, Nevill's house originally belonged to the Pre-Raphaelite watercolorist George Price Boyce, who used the drawing room as his painting studio. All of Nevill's previous homes in London have been studios, since he prefers rooms on a grand scale, with very large open spaces and high ceilings with skylights, especially when filled with the massive furniture he collects. During the fifties and sixties Nevill haunted the demolition sales of the now-defunct Victorian and Edwardian social clubs—the Conservative, the Bath, the Old Constitutional, and the Junior Carlton—acquiring the most important elements of his collection, including the enormous bookcases originally from the Conservative Club, which currently line his drawing-room wall. He had coveted West House for years. When it finally went on the market upon the death of its previous owner, Lord Salter, Nevill was living around the corner in a studio far too small for his growing collection of furniture, books, textiles, and architectural artifacts. From the first, his acquisition of West House was to be a perfect marriage of architecture and possessions.

Nevill, Professor of Textiles at the Royal College of Art and former design director of Liberty of London, admits to having what he calls "an obsessive eye for detail," which he applies, sometimes to his discomfort, to every aspect of his life. His sensibility—a preference for mellow rooms filled with accumulated objects, furniture from old buildings and estate sales, mementos from old friends, china inherited or bought from country houses, worn carpets, slightly shabby sofas, and layer upon layer of mismatched comfortable paraphernalia—is English to the core. When Nevill, whom I had never met before, greeted me at the door, his first question was: "You aren't one of those American ladies who are expecting apricot walls, are you?" Although I had been prepared for leather Chesterfields and Turkey carpets, I had not anticipated the restless creative spirit of the owner and the sheer beauty of the house itself. There was controlled chaos when we arrived. Piles of flowers lay everywhere, fresh in boxes just in from the florist and dried in bunches littering the Turkey runner in the entryway. Photographing Nevill's house was to be a bit like working with an artist as he paints a still life. Within the confines of the canvas, in this case the rooms of West House, the process of rearranging, making minute but to the owner essential changes, continually re-examining, adding, and re-creating, is the essence of decoration, a never-ending challenge. The idea is to make each room the best it can be for the moment. "For the time being," Nevill says, "it will be perfect."

Nevill insists that photographing West House is virtually pointless because it will always be in a state of change. As soon as Nevill can restore Boyce's studio to its original plan, the Conservative Club bookcases will be earmarked for the second floor, which will become the new library. The yellow wallpaper in the current drawing room will eventually be replaced by a gilded leather embossed with vines that Nevill rescued from the Imperial Institute. In the little sitting room, bits of William Morris wallpaper taped to the wall behind a Frederick Sands painting indicate Nevill's future vision for that room. In the meantime, Nevill will continue to acquire, remove, assemble, collect, paint, and build. What remains constant is the palette of West House, somber and rich, with occasional shafts of golden sunlight catching the sheen of bronze and marble, the texture of a William Morris tapestry, and the faded leather of old books.

Right: From the drawing room/library of West House, one can see the Chelsea Old Rectory garden. The mammoth Ziegler carpet that covers the floor was formerly in the library at Rudding Park. The Howard sofa, one of a pair made in 1870, was also originally at Rudding Park and is covered in pieces of eighteenth-century gros point. In front of it is a lioness skin. The gramophone was a gift from the Honorable Griselda Joynson-Hicks, who used it at the Monkey Club, a finishing school in Mitford House that she ran in the thirties. The girls at the school practiced typing to its accompaniment. The nineteenth-century tapestry curtains were formerly at Blair Drummond Castle in Perthshire. At right is one of a pair of eighteenth-century powder-blue Chinese jars. The Gothic bronze clock was made in the 1830s. The head of Ajax is also nineteenth-century bronze.

Right: From the dining room, one can also view the garden, framed by Morris Merton Abbey woven wool curtains, actually made by the firm of Morris & Co. in 1875. The heraldic damask tablecloth, twelve yards long, was originally at Croxteth Hall in Liverpool. The silverware is the nineteenth-century King's pattern, except for the pistol-handled knives, which are eighteenth-century. The glasses are a mixture of English and French from the eighteenth and nineteenth centuries. The china is nineteenth-century Mason's ironstone. The candlestick is from a set of six, originally from a nineteenth-century English convent. The gilt bronze candelabrum at the back of the room is one of a pair made in the 1860s. The light fixtures are Edwardian billiard-table lights by Thurston.

Far right: The bookcases, purchased from the Conservative Club in the 1950s, hold Nevill's extensive reference library on art and design. The nineteenth-century Howard chair is covered in seventeenth-century Jacobean crewelwork. The ladder, one of three owned by Nevill, was originally in the Times *library in Printing House Square. The library folio stand is nineteenth-century. The eighteenth-century chair on the left, one of a set of ten library chairs, is covered in gros point.*

Right: In the guest bedroom, the half-tester bed is
hung with nineteenth-
century Brussels lace. On
the bed is a Schiaparelli
evening coat in quilted
pink silk crepe with a satin
lining, made in 1936. All
furniture in the bedroom is
satinwood from the eight-
eenth, nineteenth, and
twentieth centuries, including the nineteenth-century
satinwood writing table.
(Even the lavatory, which
is not seen here, has been
boxed in pieces of nine-
teenth-century satinwood.)
The wallpaper is from a
design by Angelica Kauff-
mann, the eighteenth-
century Anglo-Swiss
painter.

Left: On the wall in the little sitting room is a portrait of Clara Flower, a frequent visitor to West House during the nineteenth century, painted by Frederick Sands in 1876, in a Rossetti frame. The horse was made by George Stubbs in plaster to be used as an artist's model. All the china is eighteenth-century blue and white K'ang-hsi. The chair in front of the inlaid Art Nouveau mirror at the right is Edwardian mahogany. The radio is from the 1950s.

P A W S O N

Right: Pawson uses his drawing board as both a worktable and, at a lower height, as a dining table. The floor is American pitch pine with two coats of ebony stain.

"Living the life" is what John Pawson calls it. Pawson, an architect whose ideas about design amount to a radical manifesto, has evolved an austere and inflexible doctrine about the way he, his family, and his clients should live. The "life" Pawson refers to is the simple life, one in which the living environment has been reduced to essentials. His concerns are aesthetic rather than spiritual, although Pawson insists that his preference for unadorned white walls and bare black floors, completely devoid of color, ornament, or decoration, is a logical choice rather than a fashionable statement. To Pawson, keeping all aspects of the home as basic as possible just makes sense. Why have a bedside table, he asks, when you can use the floor?

To the uninitiated, Pawson's design philosophy takes getting used to. Visitors to his home, which he also uses temporarily as an office, must remove their shoes, adding them to the lineup of footwear already neatly stacked against one of the white walls. The reception room, totally bare except for a Matisse drawing on one of the walls and a light placed on the shiny ebony floor, is also considered the living area. Guests are given the luxury of a *zabuton,* a kneeling mat, if they wish to sit down. At one time, all the rooms including this one had fireplaces, but Pawson considered them unnecessarily ornamental and inefficient. "We threw them away," he informs me. The only remaining architectural element aside from the walls is the structural column flanking the entrance to the kitchen. Pawson worries that the round shape might seem jarringly decorative, but admits that the column is necessary to keep the walls from collapsing.

Pawson lives with the art dealer Hester van Royen and their son. When van Royen was pregnant, she indulged herself by sleeping on three futons on the floor of the bedroom, which are stored in a closet during the day so as not to mar the clean lines of the room or make it distinguishable in any noticeable way from the living area. Usually, Pawson and van Royen sleep on one slim futon. The bedroom differs in style from the living area only in that it contains a small black television set, kept, of course, on the floor. When it is turned on the color appears almost shockingly vibrant in the ascetic environment. Pawson tells me that it is his belief that "color comes on its own." When rooms are kept as simple as possible, one notices the art on the walls and not the wall itself. "There is a finality about black," he says, "which is very satisfying."

Pawson's design doctrine extends to basic necessities like washing and cooking. The white tile bathroom contains a plain wooden box, which Pawson describes as a traditional Japanese bathtub. One must wash before entering the tub, which is used for soaking in very hot water before bed as an aid to sleep. Pawson rather ruefully admits that the chrome water spout is necessary, but wishes that for aesthetic reasons it could be eliminated. The "life" is harder to maintain in the kitchen. Pawson tells me he has tried to convince van Royen to narrow their cooking utensils down to just one pot for all cooking needs— apparently without success. The spare white kitchen cupboards hide a few stray pots and vases in addition to the unornamented white china Pawson insists upon. According to Pawson, many of his wealthier clients come to him because they want his help getting rid of a lifelong accumulation of material possessions. "They want to live a simpler life," he says, "like we do."

Right: The charcoal-on-paper drawing in the entrance room by Henri Matisse is entitled Head of a Woman. *The light, designed by Castiglione, is used throughout the flat. The* zabuton *is Japanese. The coffee cup is insulated stainless steel.*

Left: The traditional Japanese bath is cedar of Lebanon, made for Pawson in Yorkshire by Design Workshop.

Right: The Cosmic Oval at the entrance to the house announces some of its many themes in a continuous sentence stenciled above the mirrored panels. The mural, painted by William Stok, is a group portrait of some of civilization's enlightened thinkers, including Erasmus and Thomas Jefferson pictured in conversation with Hannah Arendt. Behind the figures, the painting represents the evolution of the galaxies. According to Jencks, the Cosmic Oval is designed to be pretentious—"to pretend to more knowledge and wisdom than we can possibly have." This pretension is parodied by the architect, who created a similar design in the bathroom, called the Cosmic Loo.

The Thematic House is an 1840s town house owned by the critic and architect Charles Jencks, who has renovated it into a complete environment based on symbols. Jencks, known as the critic who invented the concept of postmodernism in architecture, believes that modern architecture, born in an agnostic age, lacks meaning and historical perspective. He urges, through his writing and teaching, that aesthetics in architecture be informed by symbols so that all architectural detail has significance beyond the purely visual. Most critics think themselves lucky if their ideas are published in journals, and even luckier if those ideas are given serious consideration within their chosen field. Jencks is in the rare position of a man who has the skill, energy, and resources to execute, in homes of his own, his theories about architecture and design. The Thematic House in London is an example of what happens when a critic is able to put theory into practice.

Jencks has written a book about his London home, so we knew something about what to expect when we were admitted into the Thematic House through the Human Door, featuring an abstract representation of a human face. From the entrance, most of the ground floor—with the exception of the bathroom, called the Cosmic Loo—can be seen: a sequence of rooms based, according to Jencks, on five seasons. We wandered from room to room, from the Winter Room, into the Spring (both sitting rooms, with Spring overlooking the garden), then clockwise into Summer (the dining room), to Indian Summer (the kitchen), and to Autumn (a multifunctional room), following the cycle of time as seen by Jencks. At the core of the house, both literally and metaphorically, is the Solar Stair, a spiral staircase with fifty-two steps, representing the weeks in a year, and seven landings, for the days in the week. Walking around the stair from Autumn back into Winter, we had made the journey, symbolically, through a solar year.

Most of the symbolism in the Thematic House is abstract, and often appears at first glance to be purely decorative. Throughout the house, one sees versions of a new form invented by Jencks, which he calls the Jencksiana. His idea is that one motif, in this case a face motif created by a combination of curves and staggers, can take on many guises. Jencks, who has written extensively on anthropomorphic architecture, wanted to try out the idea of projecting bodily states onto buildings. He believes that the Jencksiana can be altered into a complete set of physiological types: "Fat and dumb, pert and silly, owl-like and solemn, straight and balanced, cat-like and surprised—the cast of characters, if not a complete human comedy, is wide." Once inside the Thematic House, we could not avoid playing Hunt the Symbol, and were soon discovering face motifs in doorways, light fixtures, chairs, and windows.

Jencks has written that skeptics who visit the Thematic House often end up reading very personal meanings into the architecture that Jencks had not intended. Although Jencks sees that as proof of an innate human desire to find meaning in architecture, perhaps these people are more intrigued by Jencks's ability to translate his own dogma into aesthetic reality. It is a mighty power to have. As a visitor I found myself appreciating the more obvious and natural aspects of the house—the warm, burnt-orange colors of the Indian Summer Kitchen, enhanced as the late-afternoon sun poured into the room—without realizing that the kitchen was designed on the theme of Hindu architecture and that "Indian" Summer was both a symbol and a pun. Jencks would argue that my mode of perception reflects the mental attitudes of this particular, spiritually sterile time in history. Most of us, unlike the ancient Egyptians, for example, are unaccustomed to reading meaning into a building. Whether right or wrong, once inside the Thematic House one cannot help but search for a meaning in all the meaning, and marvel at the energy involved in putting theory to the test.

Right: The theme of the Sun Table and Sun Chairs is summer. They are located, not surprisingly, in the Summer Room, which Jencks had painted in warm tones reminiscent of the sun's rays. The chairs have "sunburst" backs, decorated with a variation of the Jencksiana motif, and were designed to follow the body's curves. The expandable Sun Table has a globe at its center, which is echoed by the surface decoration on the tabletop.

Below: In Summer, *a painting by Allen Jones located in the Summer Room, a glowing dancer, symbolizing the season, dances to the music of Father Time, shown as an aging musician in a tree. The painting, according to Jencks, is based partly on Nicolas Poussin's* A Dance to the Music of Time.

Left: These rectangular storage units are located in the Autumn Room next to the Indian Summer Kitchen. The theme of autumn, illustrated here by the burnt-orange color, is represented more abstractly by the decorative symbols on the facade. These are meant to suggest three women carrying baskets of grapes on their heads, an image of autumn. As Jencks points out, this image is unclear unless actual grapes are put in bowls on top of the unit.

Far left: The main bed-room, called the Foursquare Room, features the square, which Jencks calls "the most ubiquitous motif in architecture," as both a structural and a decorative element. Symbolic refer-ences are made throughout the room to the number four—four elements, four ages of men, four parts of the day, four great civiliza-tions. The foursquare violet motif, used as a decorative element, was influenced by the work of the Glasgow-born architect Charles Ren-nie Mackintosh.

Left: The Moonwell is a light shaft designed to illu-minate a dark landing and a dressing room. The space appears to be cylindrical but is actually a half-circle reflected by mirrors to give the illusion of a full circle. Looking up, one sees an etching of the moon on the mirror. At night, real moonlight is reflected down the well and one can some-times see glimpses of the moon in the mirror.

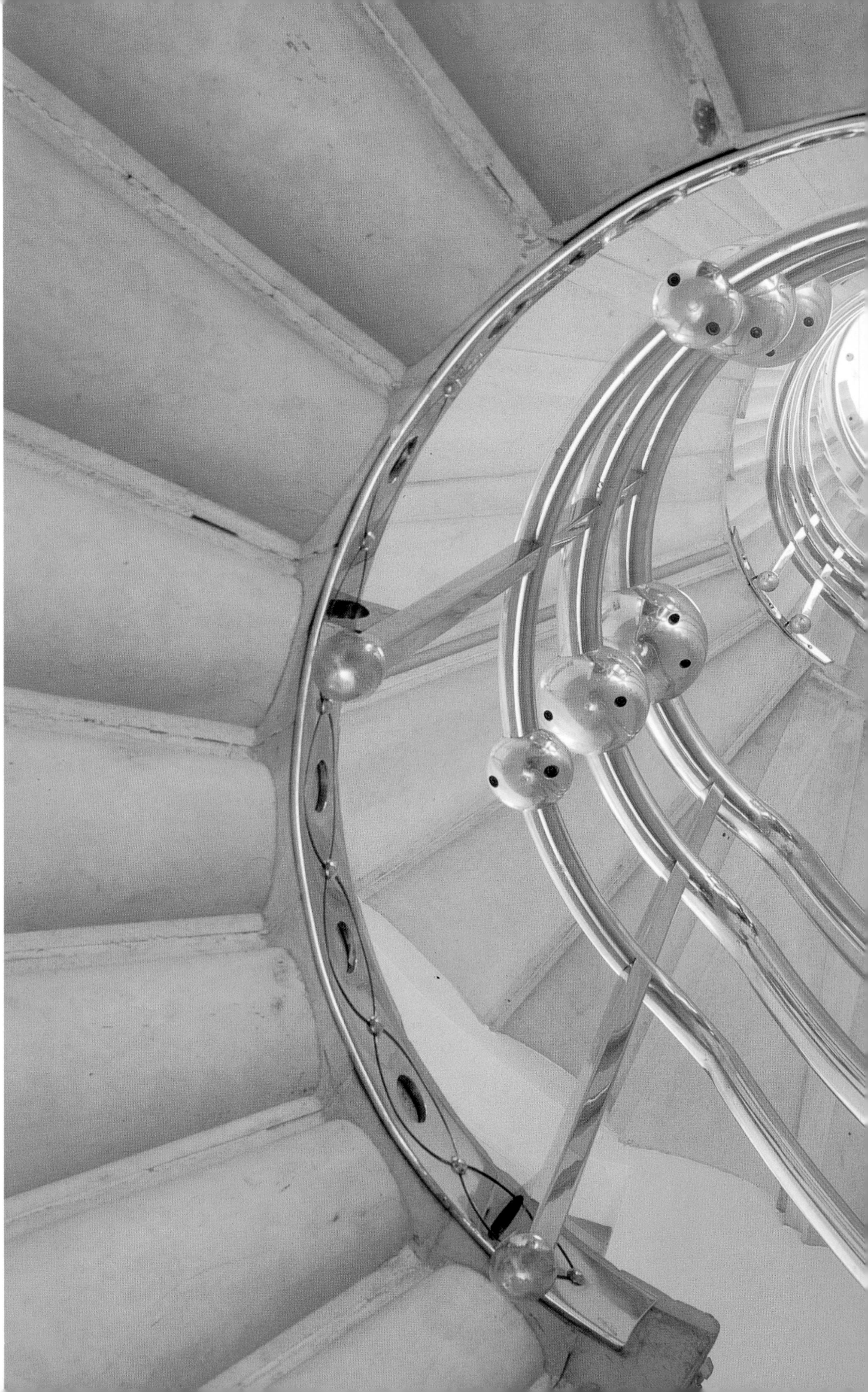

Left: From the Solar Stair, which is an abstract representation of the solar year, one can see glimpses of five rooms of the ground floor simultaneously. The light at the top of the stair symbolizes energy and hope, according to Jencks, who has called the stair "the physical and psychological center of the house."

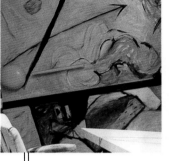

Right: The poles, found and painted red and white, are described by Connor as "sculpture." The black triangles on the floor are made from vinyl. Connor had originally intended the molding, which runs askew along the middle of the wall, to be made from spaghetti.

P I R R O N I

The idea, according to the architect and designer David Connor, was to create an environment in which conventional architectural perspective was altered. His client, Marco Pirroni, a guitarist and songwriter for the band Adam Ant, thought that was a great concept. "Dave skirted the issue for a while," Pirroni told me. "Talked about disrupting the order of things. I thought of the Aristocats—the cartoon where Tom and Jerry went to Paris and when they got there the Eiffel Tower, everything around them, was crooked. Apparently, Dave was thinking more of German Abstract Expressionism."

No one entering Marco Pirroni's flat would think of a children's cartoon. The monochromatic hues of the walls in the main room, lit from above by a large skylight, create a somber, introspective atmosphere. Odd abstract shapes are splashed across the wall in violent patterns, as if they were painted during an angry outburst. The walls appear as if they might fall down on top of you. Doors loom, floors are intentionally uneven. Connor wanted the room to be precarious, unreliable. The central table, designed by Connor with sharp corners and an aggressive, jutting shape, has a leg that protrudes out into the room. According to Connor, visitors to the room were constantly tripping, unaware of the leg because its monochromatic patterns blended with the painted walls. Connor installed another leg next to the first, which jutted even farther into the room. This leg was painted in red and white checks similar to a warning marker. "People trip over this leg also," Connor said to me with a deadpan expression, "but at least they can see what they are tripping over."

Pirroni's flat invites the obvious comparison to *The Cabinet of Dr. Caligari* not only because of the mannered shapes reminiscent of gothic patterns or the ominous mood caused by the distortion of ordinary objects. Much of the drama of the sets for Caligari also comes from the use of painted canvas, ornamentation that suggests rather than accurately represents specific emotions. Connor originally intended the walls to remain bare, relying on the irregularity of the architecture to confuse the sense of reality. Although his drawings looked bizarre, the offbeat structure of the interior seemed insubstantial and a bit silly when construction had been completed. To take the concept into a more abstract realm, Connor commissioned the Swedish sculptor Madelaine Palme to paint the walls, as well as the furniture inherited from Pirroni's previous 1950s-style flat. The walls became a creative battleground for artist, client, and architect, as Palme painted and repainted according to the various emotional desires of the three involved. Pirroni and Connor are inarticulate about the subject of the wall painting. Pirroni muttered to me that it was something "vaguely sexual," while Connor dismissed the question by telling me: "It's whatever you want it to be." It is apparent that, whatever one reads into the contradictory patterns and conflicting shapes, the subject for the walls, as well as the impetus for the flat, is anarchy, a controlled breaking of the rules.

Left: Connor intended the pink glass of the mirrored cupboard, which opens into a storage area, to be shattered, adding another element of distortion. Pirroni preferred to keep the mirror intact for practical reasons.

Right: The table, made by E. & F. Joinery and designed especially for Pirroni's flat, was painted by Madelaine Palme in artist's oils, as were the walls. On the right wall is a framed copy of the only issue of Anarchy in the UK, *published in 1976 by the rock group the Sex Pistols. The painted squares on the floor continue up the wall to heighten the impression of instability. The chairs, some painted by Palme and some covered with fake fur, are from the 1950s.*

*Right: The doorway leading
to a sun porch overlooking
the garden is an addition
to the house built under
Bennison's supervision. The
ebonized Anglo-Indian
table is flanked by nine-
teenth-century wicker
chairs. The chandelier is
nineteenth-century Russian.
The gilt-bronze statue of
Venus is nineteenth-century
French, by Albert Carrier-
Belleuse. The doorknobs are
Venetian glass.*

G O L D S M I T H

One of the endless peculiarities of upper-class British society is that while it traditionally abhors anything that even faintly hints of "trade," it admires and delights in the fact that certain English decorators like Sybil Colefax or the great Geoffrey Bennison would keep shops. Bennison's elite clientele included Lord Weidenfeld, two branches of the Rothschild family, Princess Firyal of Jordan, and a selection of Park Avenue matrons and debutante daughters of the very rich. The basement of his dusty shop in the Pimlico Road, filled with moldering fabric swatches and busts of Roman emperors, fainting couches and Empire armoires, chipped eighteenth-century Chinese vases and, at least at one time, a "lost" Poussin painting, was a gathering place for an odd assortment of society clients and antiques-world hangers-on. In certain circles, to say of a new acquisition "I just found it in Geoffrey's shop" needs no other explanation.

Bennison died before completing work on Isabel Goldsmith's town house, with the result that the house has an air of unfinished business about it. Bennison's famous style, best exemplified by the New York apartment of Baron Guy de Rothschild and his wife, Marie-Hélène, which has a cozy elegance redolent of old money and a studied lack of concern about it, has been replaced here by an elegant refinement that possibly reflects the tastes and involvement of the owner more than Bennison. Many of the pieces in the house were inherited from the Patino collection belonging to Goldsmith's grandfather, such as the antique Venetian chairs in the drawing room and the nineteenth-century faux lapis side cabinet. Other pieces, purchased before and after Bennison's death, reflect Goldsmith's passion for nineteenth-century Romanticism, especially Pre-Raphaelite painting. This is not to say that there are no traces in Goldsmith's house of the artistry of Geoffrey Bennison. The stenciling on the drawing-room walls, completed by a member of Bennison's "family"—the full-time craftspeople he employed for all his jobs—is one of Bennison's many trademarks. The draperies in the drawing room are made up of pieces of authentic William Morris fabric together with new fabric carefully woven to match the original, a classic Bennison technique. The walls are covered in original nineteenth-century paper, "rescued" by Bennison from some mysterious source. The flowered fabric that covers the four-post bed, as faded and restrained as if it had been in place since the nineteenth century, is actually modern, from the Bennison fabric shop. The only missing element is the studied shabbiness—the frayed carpets, and paint peeling from priceless antiques—so essential to the Bennison style. The quality and the attention to detail are unmistakably Bennison.

Long before the very wealthy flocked to his shop, Bennison ran a junk stall on the Portobello Road, where he acquired a reputation as the possessor of a miraculous "eye" for genuine treasures, which could be discovered among his collection of worn sofas and Victorian lampshades. As his reputation grew, he insisted on working only with people he felt a bond with, perhaps only one client a year. Rumor had it that his fees were astronomical. (Bennison would discourage more modest clients with his own Waspish version of the famous line first attributed to J. P. Morgan: "If you have to ask price, dear, you can't afford it.") Yet he supported his enormous "family" year round, which was a financial drain, and seemed to be as unconcerned with making money as if to the manner born. Toward the end, he was less available to old acquaintances and preferred to see only his grander clients. Some say that some of his last work betrays a slickness, a decorated finish, that was decidedly lacking from the quintessential Bennison interior. Nevertheless, his legacy had been inherited by the current generation of decorators in both London and New York—that anyone with self-confidence and an eye for quality can create the aura of great wealth by diligently perfecting the fantasy of how unimportant it all is.

Far left: The foreground sculpture, Mephistoph- eles, *is nineteenth-century Russian. In the background is an important painting by Edward Burne-Jones enti- tled* Pan and Psyche. *On the Chinese red and black table is a French nine- teenth-century silver and gilt-bronze sculpture enti- tled* Hebe *by Albert Carrier-Belleuse.*

Left: The painting over the fireplace in the drawing room is The Lady of Shalott *by the Pre- Raphaelite artist Sidney Mereyard. The sheep in the far corner of the room is nineteenth-century Chinese cloisonné. The Venetian chairs, from the Patino col- lection, were made by Brustalon. The nineteenth- century side cabinet, from the same collection, is faux lapis and aventurine, with rare Louis XIV style of or- molu. Above the cabinet is a Pre-Raphaelite painting by Simeon Solomon, enti- tled* Love in Autumn. *The curtains are French Napoleon III appliqué on tulle. The nineteenth-cen- tury bronze in the fore- ground by Lord Leighton is entitled* Athlete and Python. *The walls are covered with nineteenth- century paper found by Bennison.*

Right: The nineteenth-century mirror in Gold-smith's bedroom is glass mosaic from Ravenna. The silver vases on the mantel are nineteenth-century representations of Beauty and the Beast. The candleholders on the mantel are Art Nouveau. The chair in front of the window is eighteenth-century French gilt wood and leather. The walls and bed are covered in fabric made by Geoffrey Bennison.

L O

S ANGELES

Preceding pages: The terrace is located outside Midler's bedroom. The garden can be seen through her windows. The chair without a seat is a French iron patio chair.

Right: The walls of the Midler house, which were originally dark, have all been hand-painted by Nancy Kintisch. At the front door to the house are wrought-iron bells, collected by Midler and painted by Kintisch, and a bird that was a decoration from a party to celebrate the arrival of Midler's first child. The Mexican religious painting was a gift to Midler from a friend.

"Just a bunch of working artists" is the way the New York painter Nancy Kintisch describes her collaboration with Bette Midler and the decorator Jarrett Hedborg on the design and ornamentation of Midler's Beverly Hills home. Midler, says Kintisch, likes to be around other creative people. "She thrives on the energy." When Midler bought her Spanish-style Los Angeles house, which had been built in the 1920s, she had already begun to mull over the idea of artists living together and creating art in the environment. Her idea had its roots in the work of Carl Larsson, a Scandinavian artist and illustrator whose wife and children joined with him to paint the environment they lived in as part of an ongoing creative communal project. The unusual aspect of Midler's program was that it was conceived in Hollywood, land of the "star system," by a celebrated personality. "There was no ego involved," says Kintisch. "We talked, one or the other of us would come up with an idea, another might try it or reject it. Sometimes I would actually paint a wall to show it to Bette. Jarrett has had chairs re-covered to give Bette an idea of his idea. Furniture moved from room to room, colors changed. Why should there be ego? Bette is an artist."

Kintisch wasn't always this matter-of-fact about the project. She remembers arriving in Los Angeles to meet with Midler for the first time. Not knowing what to expect, she kept her taxi waiting outside. She spent only a few minutes with Midler. "Bette took me into the dining area. At that time it was dark wood, unpainted. She showed me a rose petal. 'This is what I want this room to feel like,' " Midler told Kintisch. "Then she left town to make a movie." For the most part, Midler was part of every creative decision. One night Kintisch and Midler, talking late into the night, decided to repaint Midler's bedroom, which had been repainted several times previously but not completely to their satisfaction. The two women, both wearing pajamas, drew patterns on the wall with chalk until they had blocked out the design. Then, while Kintisch painted until dawn, Midler sat in a chair offering suggestions and making comments, sharing Kintisch's thoughts as the wall mural took shape. In the living room, Midler designed the French-style doors, Hedborg the chairs and sofas, and Kintisch the antique mirrored and ceramic tile mosaic on the fireplace. "We all had a special kind of communication," says Kintisch, "on another level."

As they worked together, Kintisch, Midler, and Hedborg were to discover that they shared many of the same influences. "You want to know what inspired us?" asks Kintisch. "Cecil Beaton and the Ballets Russes of Monte Carlo and Vanessa Bell and Duncan Grant and Roger Fry, the group flavor of Bloomsbury." They also seem to share an openness, the willingness to experiment with almost any style. The pinstripe in the bedroom was from a "Finnish phase," according to Kintisch. The porch, with its faded chalky palette of gold, terra-cotta, and turquoise, was "inspired by the spirit of Nubian house decoration." The only difficulty seems to be deciding whose idea each phase was. "It's hard to say," says Kintisch, "where Bette's ideas end and where Jarrett's and mine begin."

Right: Inside the window frame, and at random intervals along the dining-room walls, Nancy Kintisch painted pale celadon-green and white checks, a pattern suggested by Midler. The chair, one of a set, was designed by Midler and finished by the California woodworker Nancy Martin Foto. The table was designed by Midler. The urn is California pottery. The pecan floor was stripped and painted to look bleached.

Left: Kintisch hand-painted the trompe l'oeil curtain on the right side of the wall in the living room. To the left is a portrait of Mary Pickford, dated 1932. On the table are a nineteenth-century Aubusson tapestry (one of a pair) patterned with tropical vegetation, an English silver bud vase, and a lamp made from a French silvered-bronze candlestick. The American hooked rug is from the early 1900s. The wall sconce was part of the original architecture of the house.

Below: The fireplace in the main living room has a mosaic base, designed and executed by Kintisch and made from Venetian glass, antique mirrored tiles, and ceramic tiles. The chimney, also a design by Kintisch, is a pattern of gold- and silver-leaf squares, painted to look "attractively tarnished." At random intervals, opal pieces are embedded in the wall. The French-style doors were designed by Midler. The andirons are copies of a Giacometti design acquired from the Rockefeller collection.

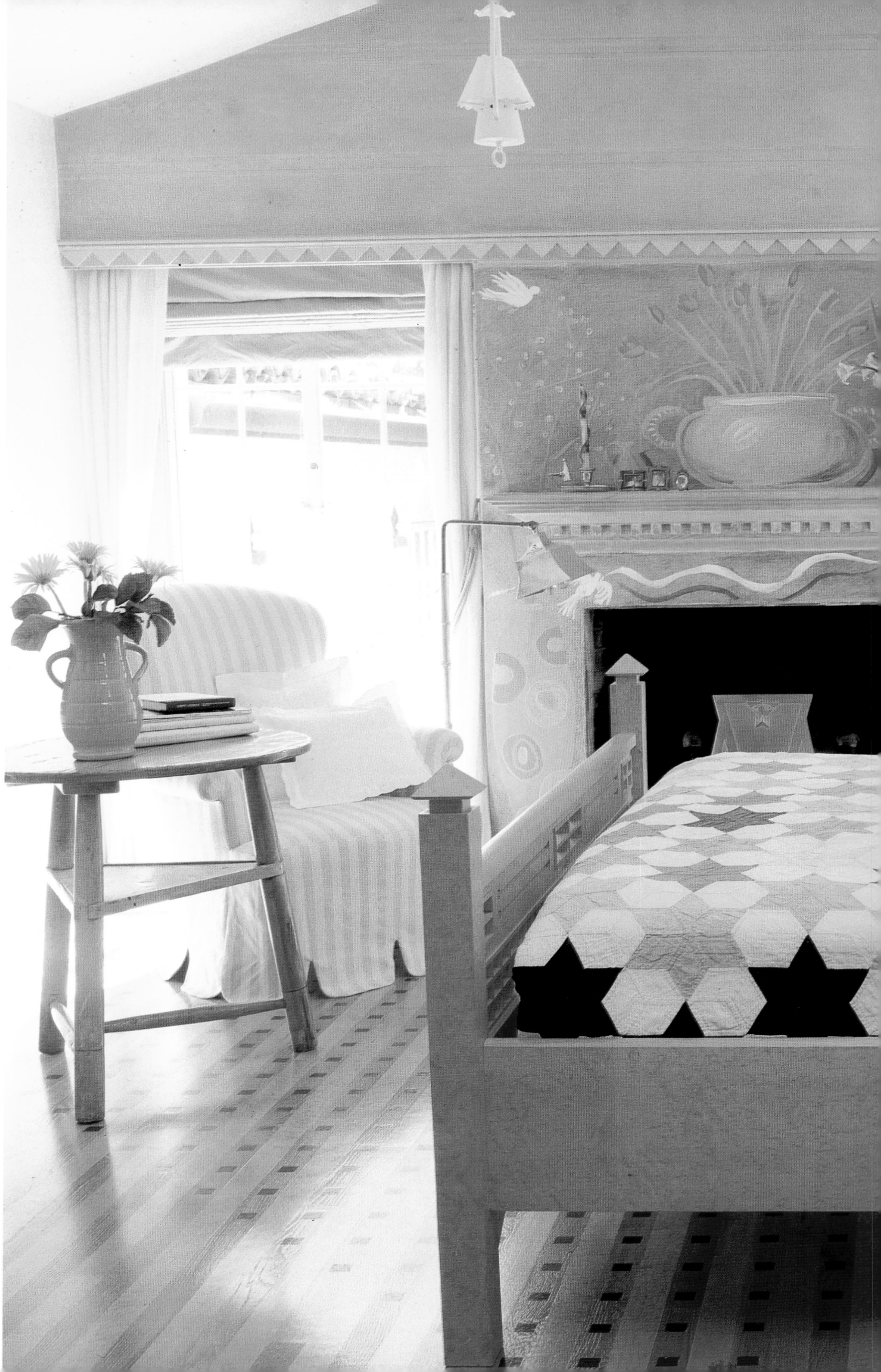

Left: The mural in the bedroom was painted by Nancy Kintisch. The bed was designed by Midler with the architect Joe Murphy in the style of Charles Rennie Mackintosh. Mackintosh was also the inspiration for the striped floor. The quilt on the bed is American, from the early part of the twentieth century.

Right: The porch has been hand-painted by Kintisch, who used a technique of applying paint over chalk to create the effect of prim-itive wall decoration. The porch swing was designed by Jarrett Hedborg and made by the craftsman Richard Mulligan.

Left: The fabric on the garden table was hand-painted by Kintisch, who also painted other fabrics for the house. The theme for this fabric was a series of "muse figures"—naked women running through a swamp. The garden furniture, like other parts of the house, has undergone several transformations. At one time it was painted to look like anodized copper.

Right: The pond, located outside the ground-floor dining area and adjoining desk area, is filled with water lilies and koi, Japanese carp that are highly prized in Japan and valued according to their markings.

Joel Silver is a Hollywood producer who owns Storer House, a restored house in the Hollywood Hills created by the architect Frank Lloyd Wright. Silver, who describes himself as a "Wright devotee," bought the house "thanks to Eddie Murphy," the actor who played the leading role in Silver's most successful movie, *48 Hours.* Silver calls Wright the greatest American artist of the twentieth century. "Wright's vision," says Silver, "is very cinematic. He created all of the elements himself. In the movies, the script, the casting, everything must be seamless. Wright worked the same way."

Storer House had been on the market for five years when Silver purchased it. Structurally, the 2,500-square-foot building was sound, but Silver had virtually no idea what the house, which had been alternately neglected and renovated over a period of sixty years, originally looked like. With the help of Eric Lloyd Wright, the architect's grandson, he began the arduous process of restoration, bringing the house back to life "from the ground up." It was a painful process because the house had been badly abused, but it was also a process of discovery. At one time, all the interior redwood and concrete had been painted black. The concrete that remained uncovered appeared yellow, the result of a sixty-year accumulation of dirt. Silver had it cleaned and restored using the original molds for any concrete sections that had to be replaced. One day, the crew working on the outside of the house discovered tubular bronze channel lamps, originally inside the house, buried in the garden, painted black and badly twisted. They are now in use on the second floor of the house.

The work of Frank Lloyd Wright seems to be, for Silver, something between a hobby and a passion. He knows all of Wright's major projects down to the littlest detail, and has incorporated his knowledge into the Storer House restoration. "I wanted the house to feel the way Wright intended it to," says Silver. Some of the pieces of furniture in the house are original Frank Lloyd Wright pieces. More often, Silver furnished with reproductions copied from pieces in Wright's Imperial Hotel in Tokyo, the Martin House in Buffalo, the Trier House in Iowa, and others. Since Wright often softened his houses with textiles and ceramics, Silver collects American pottery and glass from the early twentieth century. He employs a full-time construction supervisor, whose job it is to ensure that Storer House is always in optimum shape. Even the lily pond outside the main room on the ground floor has been restored with an almost compulsive eye for authenticity. The pond is filled with coi, "award-winning" carp that are similar to those originally found in the pool at the Imperial Hotel.

When we arrived, Silver was on the telephone next to the swimming pool, his final addition to Storer House. The pool, which had been part of the original design for the house, had never been built. Eric Wright reconstructed the design, and Silver's construction crew made four thousand concrete blocks in Silver's garage next to the house, using the original molds. "Wright," says Silver, "is the last of the great nineteenth-century philosophers, like Ford, Rockefeller, and Vanderbilt. They changed the world and made millions. Wright wanted to do the same thing. He wanted to make five thousand houses and find a way to make them both great and affordable. He wasn't able, in the end, to do that."

Right: Storer House, built in 1924, is one of eight Frank Lloyd Wright buildings in Los Angeles. The house is constructed from concrete blocks, glass, and redwood, following Wright's conception of making structure the ornament of the house. Wright designed a system that he hoped would allow relatively unskilled labor to construct unique affordable housing. A dry mix of concrete was tamped into a form to create each block, but since the blocks were not uniform the construction of each house required extremely skilled labor and became quite expensive.

Left: The table in the dining room, an original Wright piece, is from an important early Wright house of the prairie school built in 1908 in River Forest, Illinois, for Isabelle Roberts. Roberts's father was one of Wright's first benefactors. The wood is crotchy curl cypress, selected piece by piece by Wright from a part of the tree usually thrown away. The chairs are reproduced from originals in the Martin House in Buffalo. The large vase to the left is Tiffany favrile glass. The vase on the table is Clewell pottery.

Left: The original redwood beams have been restored to the unlacquered finish intended by Wright. This part of the ground floor, adjacent to the dining area, has an original Wright chair from the Trier House at the desk, designed in 1956. The rug is Chinese Art Deco, and the lamp is Roycroft copper, with a Steuben glass shade. The desk has a collection of objects from the period in which the house was constructed.

Right: Lloyd Wright, the son of Frank Lloyd Wright and the architect of Sowden House, designed the oak table and chairs in 1926. On the table are a Tiffany lamp and a Grueby vase, from Silver's collection of American pottery from the early twentieth century.

*Right: The sculptural han-
dle to Wosk's studio is a
design by Peter Shire. The
hat stand is from the
1950s. In the mirror is a
reflection of Wosk's studio
wall. The elevator door was
designed by Wosk, who
hand-painted it.*

"If there is a surface anywhere, I'll decorate it," says Miriam Wosk, the owner of a penthouse duplex apartment in Beverly Hills designed by the architect Frank Gehry. Wosk is a painter and decorative artist who uses unconventional materials, such as sequined antique dresses and gilded leather, as integral parts of her artwork. The apartment, which was a collaborative effort between Wosk, who decorated the interior, and Gehry, began as "a modest remodeling." Wosk called Gehry in 1984, attracted by the shapes of his spaces. "He seduced us with grandiose ideas," Wosk recalls, "and the opportunity to collaborate. He had an ego big enough to accept my vision." Gehry first achieved notoriety in the architecture world with his unconventional renovation of a simple suburban colonial house, Gehry House, which broke almost every rule about function, comfort, and traditional beauty in residential housing. Gehry House is considered the pioneer example of New Wave architecture in the eighties in Los Angeles. As Wosk sees it, both she and Gehry share a complex view about architecture, but hers is a more feminine vision. "He is tough, more of a chain-link-fence sensibility," says Wosk. "I brought color and pattern to the structure."

Wosk sees her apartment as a composite of all her fantasies about living in Los Angeles. She compares the design to the feeling of driving down Hollywood Boulevard or another major L.A. thoroughfare. "You see a car wash with turquoise pillars, and then the Ali Baba Motel . . . you're bombarded by color on all sides. I wanted a certain baroque richness inside the place I live." The collaborative process involved dispute and compromise. Gehry vehemently opposed the idea of a pink facade. Wosk won that battle. "Having a pink house was part of my fantasy about living in California." Gehry persuaded Wosk to accept the "fish-scale" turquoise tiles that run down the side of the building, echoing some of Gehry's other designs that have fish references. When the project began, Wosk brought Gehry pictures of various structures that appealed to her, and he tried to incorporate as many of these different architectural references into his design as possible. "There were lots of pictures of greenhouses," says Wosk, which served as models for the dining room. To Wosk the kitchen resembles a Moorish temple, and she sees her studio as "something like an airplane hangar." Together Gehry and Wosk designed the fireplace to mirror the skyscrapers in Century City, which can be seen from the living room, dining room, and terrace.

Wosk does not differentiate between her roles as artist and as decorator. She describes her style as eclectic, "everything from the work of Gaudí, who obviously was an influence, to Memphis chairs and Art Deco." Like Gehry, who has often noted the influence of such artists as Richard Serra and Claes Oldenburg on his work, Wosk was determined to incorporate the work of other artists into her own environment. The Los Angeles artist Peter Shire created a number of architectural details, such as the sculptural handles to the studio door and the ornate stereo cabinet. For Wosk, the art of decoration is "just like making a collage. It's a balancing act between color, shapes, strange materials, textures, and, of course, fantasy."

Left: As one looks up at the Wosk duplex, the greenhouse-like structure of the dining room is visible. On the left are the "fish-scale" decorative tiles designed by Gehry. In the corner of the terrace, partially obscured by the rail, is an oversized bust of David.

Right: The living room, overlooking Century City, features Wosk's collection of American Art Deco furniture, including Art Deco ponyskin couches and a piano from the first-class lounge of the SS Corona, made of inlaid blond wood. On the modern coffee table, from Atelier International, is an Art Deco vase made from blue mercury glass. The pieces on the mantel are a series of teapots by the Los Angeles artist Peter Shire, who also created the orb in the center. On the piano is a display rack from the 1950s and two Carmen Miranda vases from the forties. In the foreground are pillows, hand-painted on gold leather by Wosk, who also painted the large decorative panel on the back wall. The pot holding the palm is mosaic work by Wosk. The rug is a Juan Gris design made in Spain. The figures in front of and behind the sofas are carved wooden cigarette stands.

Right: The mosaic horse sculpture was found by Wosk in the window of Gump's department store. It was made from shards of broken Gump's teapots. The pink mirrored pots are from Mexico. The ceramic tile on the terrace, which circles the penthouse level of the apartment, was designed by Wosk, using tiles left over from other parts of the renovation.

Left: The dining room, designed to resemble a greenhouse, features a verde marble table designed by Wosk encircled by a group of First chairs by Michele de Lucchi of Memphis. The mosaic bench and chair on the terrace were designed and built by Marlo Bartel, a Laguna Beach artist. The table is shaped like an artist's palette, a favorite symbol of Wosk's.

Far left: Wosk was influenced by the Spanish/Mexican tile work seen in the Los Angeles area when she designed the tiles for the stairs, which lead from the third floor to the penthouse. The colors were chosen because they were reminiscent of "old California pottery," such as Bauer pottery, which Wosk collects.

Left: The painting, by Wosk, called The Emperor's New Clothes, *is acrylic and is collaged with sequined fabric from the 1940s. The neon is also a design by Wosk. The yellow pole is part of a stereo and television cabinet designed by Peter Shire.*

S O U R C E S

Ambasz, Emilio. *The Architecture of Luis Barragán*. New York: Museum of Modern Art, 1976.

The Andy Warhol Collection. New York: Sotheby's, catalog, April 1988.

Arwas, Victor. *Art Deco*. New York: Harry N. Abrams, 1980.

Bofill, Ricardo. *Taller de Architectura*. New York: Rizzoli, 1985.

Fonteyn, Margot. *Margot Fonteyn: Autobiography*. London: W. H. Allen, 1975.

Horn, Richard. *Memphis: Objects, Furniture, and Patterns*. Philadelphia: Running Press/Quarto, 1985.

Jencks, Charles. *Towards a Symbolic Architecture*. London: Academy Editions, 1985.

Nureyev, Rudolf. *Nureyev: An Autobiography with Pictures*. London: Hodder & Stoughton, 1962.

Percival, John. *Nureyev*. New York: Popular Library, CBS Publications, 1977.

Tarrago, Salvador. *Gaudí*. Barcelona: Editorial Escudo de Oro, 1987.

Thorndyke, John. *The Very Rich*. New York: American Heritage Publishing Co., 1976.